"I love you, Nathan. I don't want to lose you."

His expression softened, and he caressed her cheek. "I'll do my best to come back to you. But if I don't, don't wait. Take your passport and go live your life the way that you were meant to. Protecting you has been my primary mission, and if I fail at that, I might as well take a bullet to the head, because life wouldn't be worth living."

"Don't you say your goodbyes. Not yet." Jaci wiped her eyes, her gaze narrowing as she pulled herself together. "I'm going to chase the bad guys with you. I'd rather die with you than live a lifetime alone without you."

"Jaci, you don't know what you're saying...."

"Like hell I don't. I know what I want, and if you're telling me this is what you need to do in order to start a new life with me, then let's get it over with. Hopefully, when it's all over, we both end up on the other side—alive."

Dear Reader,

I love alpha heroes—there, I said it! Why? That's easy. I love the way they scream for redemption all the while pushing away every single person who could possibly redeem them. My toes curl as they turn all that pain and raw emotion inward so that no one can possibly see how much they truly hurt inside. And I sigh with delight when that one special woman manages to transform her alpha guy into someone she could actually bring home to family.

Nathan Isaacs is my favorite kind of alpha—emotionally broken, fiercely protective and desperately trying not to love the heroine. To me, that's just plain delicious!

I hope you enjoy my hard-hearted alpha hero and his perfect woman as they fight the enemy from all sides, as well as fight off their attraction to one another.

Hearing from readers is a special joy. Please feel free to drop me a line via email through my website at www.kimberlyvanmeter.com or through snail mail at Kimberly Van Meter, P.O. Box 2210, Oakdale, CA 95361.

Happy reading!

Kimberly

THE SNIPER

Kimberly Van Meter

HARLEQUIN® ROMANTIC SUSPENSE

Recycling programs for this product may not exist in your area.

ISBN-13: 978-0-373-27839-8

THE SNIPER

This edition published by arrangement with Harlequin Books S.A.

For questions and comments about the quality of this book, please contact us at CustomerService@Harlequin.com.

Printed in U.S.A.

Books by Kimberly Van Meter

Harlequin Romantic Suspense

†*Sworn to Protect* #1666
†*Cold Case Reunion* #1669
A Daughter's Perfect Secret #1696
The Sniper #1769

Silhouette Romantic Suspense

To Catch a Killer #1622
Guarding the Socialite #1638

Superromance

The Truth About Family #1391
**Father Material* #1433
**Return to Emmett's Mill* #1469
A Kiss to Remember #1485
**An Imperfect Match* #1513
**Kids on the Doorstep* #1577
**A Man Worth Loving* #1600
**Trusting the Bodyguard* #1627
****The Past Between Us* #1694
****A Chance in the Night* #1700
****Secrets in a Small Town* #1706
******Like One of the Family* #1178
******Playing the Part* #1802
******Something to Believe In* #1826

†Native Country
*Home in Emmett's Mill
**Mama Jo's Boys
***Family in Paradise

Other titles by this author
available in ebook format.

KIMBERLY VAN METER

wrote her first book at sixteen and finally achieved publication in December 2006. She writes for the Harlequin Superromance and Harlequin Romantic Suspense lines. She and her husband of seventeen years have three children, three cats and always a houseful of friends, family and fun.

Chapter 1

Jaci Williams hadn't always been a party girl, but after a night of body shots and now puking her guts out in the alley behind Ricochet, who would believe her?

The truth was, sometimes a girl would do anything to blot out a memory—including killing multiple brain cells with tequila and lime.

"Hold on, there, *chica,*" her best friend and partner in crime slurred as she tried to keep Jaci from falling into the muddy muck that reeked of bad decisions and too many free drinks from guys hoping to get lucky. "If you go face-first in that garbage, you're on your own," Sonia warned, trying to keep Jaci steady. "You done? Or do you need to go another round?"

Jaci wiped her mouth and offered a sloppy grin. "I'm good. Where's the cab? I'm ready to go to bed."

"Not down this creepy alley, that's for sure," Sonia managed to quip as they helped each other down the uneven pavement, stumbling a few times. "We should've left through the front door. They have cabs lined up, ready to go. But no, you wanted to go out the back door so no one saw you throw up. Jaci, I swear to God, if I get jumped or raped, I'm going to kick your ass."

Jaci smiled, feeling somewhat better, if not totally steady on her feet after unloading an excess of liquor onto the dirty ground. Ricochet was their favorite club and Fridays it was always hopping. Both Jaci and Sonia loved to dance and drink, two activities that Ricochet honored with plenty of loud music and even more alcohol.

"Did you see that guy totally checking you out?" Sonia said as they walked arm in arm down the dark path. The lights from the street glittered in the pale moonlight as the nightlife dwindled to nothing in the early-morning hours. The Los Angeles heat was still oppressive, causing Jaci's skin to prickle with sweat. She pushed her hair from her eyes and tried to remember who Sonia was talking about. She simply shrugged when she couldn't recall.

Sonia nudged her in the arm. "Come on, you can't tell me you didn't notice him. Tall, dark and a little dangerous-looking, actually," Sonia said with a happy shiver. "The kind who'll at least buy you dinner before having his way with you."

Jaci kept her thoughts to herself on that score. She'd

known a man like that and while the sex had been incredible, he'd snapped her heart in two and left it a bloody mess without once looking back. Sonia exhaled, adding, "Well, I thought for sure he was going to buy you a drink but he left about an hour ago. Sorry, kid. He might've been The One."

Doubtful, Jaci thought, but smiled anyway. "Stop trying to find my Mr. Right," she murmured on a hiccup. "There are no Mr. Rights, only Mr. Right Nows and Mr. You'll Do For the Nights. Remember?"

"Right," Sonia said with mock seriousness. "Whatever you say."

They giggled, their laughter echoing in the still, closed-in heat, with Jaci's thoughts happily soaked in tequila, drowning anything that resembled regret or sadness. This was the way to get over a broken heart, she thought giddily. Who needed therapy when you had good friends and even better liquor?

They were nearly to the curb when a form stepped out from the shadow. Jaci and Sonia startled at the hulking man's sudden appearance. The alcohol in Jaci's stomach curdled with apprehension, something setting off her internal sensors to be wary. Sonia, however, suffered from no similar sense of caution and before Jaci could shoot her a warning look, Sonia reacted with irritation.

"Hey, you're blocking the way," Sonia said, motioning for him to let them pass. When he didn't budge, she yelled, "Hey, *stupido,* get out of the way. Are you deaf or something?"

"Let's just go around," Jaci muttered, pulling on Sonia's arm. "This feels weird."

"Weird is right," Sonia agreed with a glower as she pulled her pepper spray free. "You see this? It's called pepper spray and you're about to get an eyeful if you don't get the hell out of our way."

"Jaci Williams..." The man's voice was rough and sounded as if he gargled with gravel. Then he grinned, and Jaci's blood chilled. Who the hell was he? Why did he know her name? Nothing good could come of this little tableau in the making.

Sonia sucked in a sharp gasp and her hand tightened around Jaci's as he pulled a 9 mm gun with a silencer screwed onto the top. *Oh, God.* Adrenaline chased away the remnants of her intoxication and she struggled to breathe.

"You can have our money, our credit cards, whatever you want. Just let us go," Jaci pleaded, swallowing a bubble of fear burning her throat and tasting like tequila shooters. "Please..." Seconds later a tight popping sound ripped through the air and Sonia's grip on Jaci's hand loosened as she toppled to the filthy alley floor without a sound, a single bullet wound still sizzling around the torn flesh of her forehead. Her sightless eyes gazed up at the stars as blood dribbled from the wound, and it took a full second for Jaci to realize her best friend had just been shot and killed right beside her.

Jaci opened her mouth to scream as the man switched his aim and pointed the gun directly at her own head. *I'm going to die in this dirty alley.* The cops would find two corpses in the morning, stiff and gray, and that would be the end of things. Tears welled in Jaci's eyes right before she squeezed them shut. She didn't want to see the bullet coming at her. She hoped it didn't hurt too much…

Her eyes snapped open when, instead of a bullet burying itself in her brain, she heard a grunt and the distinct sound of bodies hitting the ground. Two men—the man who'd shot Sonia and another man—grappled for the gun. The other stranger landed a clean uppercut, smashing the man's jaw and shattering teeth as they clattered against each other. It was all he needed to gain the upper hand. With a quick and deadly motion, he pistol-whipped the man unconscious, and then wasted little time in splattering his brains all over the pavement.

Jaci jumped, torn between her desire to run and her need to stay with Sonia's body at least until the authorities arrived, but her savior didn't give her the choice. "Come with me," he ordered tersely and she could only stare.

"Who are you?" she asked, scared out of her mind. "What's going on? Did you know this man? Are you a cop? He just stood in our way and then he shot Sonia," she babbled, her gaze dropping to her friend's lifeless body. She cried out in shocked agony at the sheer senselessness of the crime and lowered herself to Sonia's side, clinging to the only protocol that seemed appropriate for such a horrifying situation. "We have to call 911," she said, crying openly. "We have to make a statement...we—"

"There's nothing we can do for your friend. We have to leave now," he cut in, jerking her to her feet. "That man was hired to kill you. Your friend was collateral damage. They will send another as soon as they discover this one failed. We have to take cover. Now."

"What are you talking about?" Jaci asked, wiping at her tears and staring at the man shrouded in the shadows. "Who are you? And what people are trying to kill me? I'm no one. I swear it. This is a terrible mistake. I've never even had a parking ticket."

The man stepped out of the shadow and the street lamp revealed the angled, achingly familiar and devastatingly handsome face of the man who'd ruined her for all other men and had set her on the path of destruction without a care. "Jaci...come with me, now."

"Nathan?" The name slipped from her lips like the lyrics of a song she'd never forgotten, from shock at coming face-to-face with the man who'd broken her heart so callously two months ago. "What are you doing here?"

"There's no time to explain," he answered brusquely, motioning her with a curt movement. "Let's move."

New tears burned her eyes, but these weren't tears of grief and horror. Those would come again later. The tears beginning to course down her cheeks were of pain and anger, hatred and humiliation. She'd rather die than accept a finger's worth of help from him.

"Screw you, Nathan." She didn't want him to save her. Anyone but him. "I'll take my chances."

His mouth firmed in a tight line, plainly displeased with her answer. "Not an option," he said, shocking her. Quick as a snake, he twisted her into his arms and plunged something sharp into her neck.

Then there was nothing.

Nathan Isaacs never wasted time weighing the means against the ends. The situation was simple: he wasn't leaving without Jaci, no matter if she agreed or not.

Which is why he'd come prepared with a syringe filled with a heavy sedative.

He hefted Jaci's limp body and ignored the way her tight skirt rode her thighs and exposed entirely too much leg. His grip tightened on her body, but otherwise, he kept his gaze sharp and wary. His only intent was getting her to safety. Besides, he didn't need to see what he could plainly remember.

Nathan had no trouble recalling those long legs or those full breasts. Hell, they were imprinted on his brain, likely seared into his soul. He remembered with painful clarity the way her green eyes lit up with laughter and how she had a tendency to chew her lip when worried. He'd memorized every line of her body, every frown line in her forehead.

He flashed back to the taste of her flesh in his mouth, the sound of her breathy cries when she'd reached her climax.

Oh, yes, Nathan's recollection was crystal clear in that regard.

The memories of their time together fueled his nightmares and teased his dreams.

He hadn't left her behind because he'd lost interest; he'd left her behind to save her.

And yet trouble had gone looking for her just the same.

Someone wanted her dead.

Because of him.

"I'm sorry, Jase," he muttered, laying her gently in the backseat of his car. "I never wanted my life to come after you. It wasn't supposed to be like this."

Fat lot of good his apologies and grand gestures did them both now. An innocent woman was dead and Nathan was going to have to convince Jaci to let him protect her until he could find other means.

Well, by the time the sedative wore off, they'd be long gone, deep into the Los Padres high country.

And there wasn't much she'd be able to do about that by then.

She was going to be pissed—but alive.

That's all that mattered.

Chapter 2

Jaci's head throbbed in time with the beat of her heart and her mouth tasted as if someone had stuffed it with an oily rag. She dragged her hand across her lips, still a bit sluggish in the brain, and tried to get her bearings.

Birds.

She could hear the shrill chatter of birds somewhere. She struggled to open her eyes and when she managed to peer blearily about at her surroundings, she realized with a frightening start that she had absolutely no idea where the hell she was.

Bright morning sunlight streamed in through a dusty window and the air in the room smelled musty, as if the place had been closed up for a while and only recently reopened.

Her neck ached as if someone had pinched her and

as she rubbed at the sore flesh, she recalled bits and pieces of the previous night with horrifying detail.

Sonia. Dead.

Her hand flew to her mouth and she sucked back a wild sob. How had the evening taken such a devastating turn? One minute they'd been enjoying a nice buzz from too many drinks sent their way and the next her best friend since junior high was dead. It was all too much to take in without dissolving into a moaning, sobbing mess. She wasn't the kind of woman to break into hysterics under most circumstances but she was fairly certain she was about to have a grand-level freak-out any moment as the last thread holding her nerves together frayed in spectacular fashion.

Jaci blindly fumbled around her, searching for her cell phone. She had to call the police and report it. What time was it? Likely they'd already found Sonia's body, left behind in that alley like trash. God forgive her, she'd left her best friend alone. Where the hell was her damn phone?

"If you're looking for your cell, I tossed it," came Nathan's voice from the doorway, his tone matter-of-fact and brooking no argument. He held two steaming coffee mugs in his hands but even as his gesture may have appeared kind given the circumstance, Jaci didn't know how to accept his offer considering their history.

She stared, unable to process everything at once, as Nathan walked into the room, bare to the waist, wearing faded jeans, offering a short explanation. "Your phone has a GPS and is traceable. Sorry, but I had no choice but to ditch it. Besides, you shouldn't be contacting anyone until I know it's safe to do so. In the meantime you are going off the grid."

"What the hell is going on?" she whispered, scooting away from him, rejecting his offer of coffee, though she sorely needed it. She clutched a pillow to her chest, as if that would protect her from him, and glared through a sheen of tears. "Someone shot my best friend and he was going to shoot me. You show up and k-kill that man and then kidnap me for some reason when two months ago, you couldn't stand to be near me another second. I don't understand what is happening," she couldn't help but cry with a pathetic mewl that would've embarrassed her if she hadn't been suffering from shock. "I'm in a nightmare and I can't wake up. God, help me," she said, sniffing back tears. "She's dead. Sonia is dead." Even as she murmured the words and knew it to be true, the reality felt forced.

"I'm sorry about your friend," Nathan said with genuine remorse that confused her. "I hadn't realized that the two of you had slipped out the back into the alley or else I would've been there sooner."

She regarded him slowly, recalling a snippet of Sonia's bawdy comments from that night. Why hadn't she realized it earlier? The classic jawline, the hard body built with layer upon layer of muscle… "You were the one watching us?"

He offered a curt nod but didn't deign to explain, which only made her want to throw something at his damnably handsome face.

"Why?" The inscrutable expression etched on the hard planes of his face gave nothing away and she looked elsewhere in disgust. "Right. More secrets. That's you, isn't it? Always hiding something. Well, as you so clearly stated when we last met, I mean nothing to you, so please take me home. The police can protect me from whoever is trying to kill me."

"Jaci, you're not leaving," he said, shooting her down without apology. "And don't even try. We're deep in the Los Padres Mountains. You'd never make it out alive."

"How did..." Jaci stopped in confusion, forcing her brain to work when it remained sluggish from the night before. The last she remembered she was in Los Angeles. Now she was in the mountains? She stared at Nathan, demanding answers, but when her hand strayed to the sore spot on her neck she knew the answer and her stare narrowed in indignation. "You drugged me." Neither a question nor a guess, he didn't bother denying it. She nearly shook with impotent rage. "You bastard," she swore softly under her breath. "How dare you. Who do you think you are?"

"Who am I? I'm the man who saved your life. Try to remember that fact when you're calling me a bastard. You can thank me later. For now we need to lay low. The people who want to kill you won't stop until they've achieved their objective."

"Why?" she cried, hating all this confusion and subterfuge that had nothing to do with her. "Why is this happening? I'm a graphic designer, for crying out loud. I design advertising and T-shirts and coffee mugs. What did I ever do to deserve this?"

Her impassioned cry elicited a flicker of emotion, regret, possibly, she couldn't be sure, but he shut it down quickly. "This isn't about you, Jaci," he admitted tersely before walking from the room. "It's about me."

Nathan cursed under his breath as he removed himself from Jaci's accusing stare and teary eyes. He was a bastard all right, but at least she was alive and he meant to keep her that way, even if she hated him.

He shouldn't have left the bar to do a perimeter check but he'd been sitting on that bar stool for too long, watching every jerk in the seedy club try to sleaze their way into Jaci's panties with the copious number of drinks sent her way. Not that he blamed the sorry saps—Jaci was hotter than hell on a summer day—but he didn't have any grace when it came to his former flame. She was a topic of discussion that was off-limits. He was like a wounded bear with something in its paw, and that something was a certain leggy redhead who sang off-key and danced in her underwear when she thought she was alone.

He scrubbed at the stubble on his chin and poured his second cup of coffee, knowing he'd need it to get through the next few hours alone with the one woman who knew him better than anyone on this planet—and who likely wanted to scratch his eyes out.

He didn't blame her. Not one bit. He probably deserved worse.

Good God, he could still see her stricken expression, could still picture the blood draining from her face as he deliberately broke her heart in the cruelest way he could imagine.

"You suck in bed and I'm bored. I thought I could play house but it's just not working out and I'm ready to move on. Sorry."

"You said we were going to get a place together. I've already let my apartment go and we've put a deposit down on a house! What are you talking about?"

"What can I say.... I've changed my mind."

"What am I supposed to do? Live in my car?"

"That's not really my problem, babe."

Nathan squeezed his eyes shut to block out the memory but it was seared into his synapses, punishment for believing that a normal life had been possible for a blackhearted son of a bitch like himself. He'd been deliberately cruel so that she would never want to see his face again.

He was a killer—not a suburban husband who held barbecues and shared beers with the neighbors.

And Nathan had been recklessly foolish to believe otherwise.

When his past had caught up to him, Nathan knew the safest place for Jaci would be far from him and the only way to ensure that she never wanted to see him again was to break her heart into so many pieces, she'd never be able to repair it for him.

So he'd done exactly that.

And it had worked.

Damn. His breath caught in his throat. *It had worked.*

He peered out the dusty window across the miles and miles of forest and wondered how long they'd have to hole up here before they both went stir-crazy or straight-up killed one another out of boredom.

At least here they were safe, he thought grimly, casting a short look toward the room where Jaci remained, likely in shock from seeing her best friend die a grisly death right in front of her, and wondered how he was going to protect her when he didn't even know who wanted her dead.

He turned sharply at the soft creak of the floorboard, his hand going to the Glock tucked into his waistband. Jaci jumped at his quick and unerring movement to his gun. Her gaze communicated everything he knew she was feeling—fear, anger, grief, confusion—and he supposed he had to give her some kind of explanation, though the idea ranked really low on his Excited To Do list.

"What's going on?" she asked, attempting to appear strong. But Nathan caught the subtle shake in her body. He stuffed his impulse to pull her into his arms and shelter her from anything that might harm her. *Right. Like she'd let you anywhere near her,* a voice mocked, and he grimaced at the truth of it. He watched her enter the room on unsteady feet to sit on the edge of the worn, '70s-era sofa as if she were a bird perched on a branch. "What's happening? Who was that man who k-killed Sonia?" she asked in a strained voice.

"I don't know who the man was," he admitted. "Just that you were his target."

"How did you know I was his target?" Jaci asked, her eyes wide. "Why would I be *anyone's* target?"

Because of me, he thought bitterly. But how much should he tell her? She might be safer if she knew little. "I intercepted the kill order," he said, deciding to go with honesty. She stared hard, her eyes widening even more as she shook her head as if in denial. "Jaci, there are things you don't know about me..."

"I think that was made abundantly clear several months ago," she murmured, glancing away. Her quiet comment struck him in the heart and he actually winced. Yeah, he deserved that one. She returned her gaze to him, her eyes dry and hard. "Go on."

Nathan met her gaze without flinching, yet inside he was grimacing, wishing this conversation never had to happen. "I'm not an FBI agent," he said. "I never was—it was my cover story."

"Cover story?" she repeated slowly, her tone betraying her disbelief. "What do you mean *cover* story?"

"I work for an underground government agency that specializes in neutralizing terrorist targets."

She digested this information with less shock than he'd envisioned and he was actually impressed when she didn't immediately fall apart. "When you say neutralize—"

"I'm an assassin," he cut in sharply, leaving no room for misunderstandings. Might as well just put it out there. Her life was in danger— she'd earned the truth, at the very least. "I'm trained to kill people, Jaci. It's what I'm good at and what I enjoy."

She sucked in a tiny inhale at his admission. Maybe he ought to clarify… "Listen, it's not that I *enjoy* killing people. But the assignments I get aren't good people like you and people you know. They're bad people—people who wouldn't think twice about mowing down a schoolyard of kids or torturing old folks—so when I take one out, I feel a certain satisfaction that I've done a job that needed doing." He sounded pathetic. Why was he explaining his job to a civilian who would never understand? Jaci was a bleeding-heart type. She believed in innocent until proven guilty, whereas he believed in shooting first and asking questions later. They were polar opposites on the most extreme scale. "I don't expect you to understand," he said. "But I do expect you to trust me to do what I need to, to keep you alive."

"Trust?" she said, laughing as if amused, though in truth the sound put a sick roll in his stomach. He heard her incredulity at his use of the word and he realized he should've phrased it differently. She'd never trust him, ever again. Jaci could've thrown that in his face but she didn't. Instead she said, "I think I've reconsidered your offer of coffee. Would you mind?"

"Sure," he said gruffly and went to fill her a fresh mug. He remembered that she liked it sweet with milk and sugar and without wasting time in pretending that he didn't, he simply fixed it and handed the mug to her. She accepted with a murmured thanks but otherwise remained silent as she sipped her coffee, her eyes closed as if needing a moment to collect herself. He didn't blame her; it was a lot to accept in a short time frame.

"What about Sonia?" she asked. "I need to call the police and give a statement or something, don't I?"

"I can't trust the police with your location. There are leaks everywhere. I already made an anonymous call. Your friend was picked up."

At the mention of Sonia her eyes filled but she looked away, not wanting him to see her cry. He appreciated that she was trying to stay strong but her pain caused a shaft of agony through his chest that only served to remind him that he was far from over her. "I'm sorry about your friend," he said, feeling useless in the face of her closed-in grief. Jaci accepted his condolences with a short nod and then returned to her coffee. "And I'm sorry I had to drug you," he added. "Do you need some aspirin?"

She cast him a cool look, yet nodded. He searched a few cabinets before he found what he was looking for and then shook two tablets into her hand. Her palm curled around the medicine but she didn't toss them back right away. Instead she looked his way and he was pinned by the same eyes that haunted his dreams and made him wish he'd been a better man.

"I suppose I should thank you," she began, swallowing as though the words were stuck in her throat. "For saving my life. But as much as I'm grateful…I have to wonder why you care at all. It's not as if we parted on good terms. I don't understand how I haven't spoken two words to you in months yet you happen to show up at some bar that I'm at to save my life and then bring me here—wherever *here* is—to do what? Hide out? Until when? What now? We can't stay here forever. I have a life…and it no longer includes you. That's the way you wanted it, remember? I just don't understand, Nathan."

Valid questions. She was a smart woman. But to answer truthfully? That he always knew where she was since the day he'd pretended to kick her to the curb; that he'd never forgotten a moment of their time together and the memories were both painful and treasured? That he'd wished a million times over that they'd met in a different life so that maybe they'd have had a chance? Hell, no. He couldn't say any of those things.

She peered at him closely, needing answers. "Nathan?"

And he couldn't give them without making the conscious choice to be straight with her about every facet of their former life together. She would just have to be content with the information he was willing to share. Besides, keeping her alive was his objective—not baring his soul and begging for her forgiveness.

Chapter 3

"Nathan?" The strain in her voice was evident as she stared at him, almost begging him for answers, but she could tell by the tight press of his lips that she'd have better luck prying open the vault doors at Fort Knox. "Fine. Keep your secrets. But if you can't give me a straight answer as to why I would be safer here with you than with the police, then I'm going to walk out that door and keep going until I find a road. I refuse to sit here like a little mouse under your thumb just because you say so. It's been a while since we've spent any time together so let me remind you—I don't blindly follow orders just because someone tells me to. Either start talking, or I start walking. Plain and simple."

"Jaci, don't be stupid. I do remember a few details

about our time together and one of those details is that you suck at direction. You have no idea where you are and you'll likely end up in a ravine before you find a road. Do yourself a favor and just stay put."

"No." She glared when he did a short double take at her blunt refusal. He bracketed his lean hips with his hands and returned her glare. Other people might've cowered in the face of that commanding stare but Jaci was neither cowed nor intimidated by Nathan Isaacs. "You can glower at me all day. It won't change a damn thing. I deserve answers and if you're not going to give them to me, then I'd rather take my chances out there than here with a man who thinks it's okay to treat me like a child."

"I'm trying to save your life," he said, his voice low and tense. "Don't let our past cloud your judgment. I'm the one person who can keep you safe."

"Why?" she shot back, not willing to back down. "I'm sure the police are trained to protect people. Why does it have to be you, Nathan?"

A wealth of unsaid conversations, of angst and regret, pain and shame shimmered in his dark eyes, momentarily taking her breath away at the stark exposure. But within a heartbeat he shuttered his gaze with a barked answer. "Because that's just the way it is, Jaci. Deal with it. You're not leaving. End of story. And if you try, I will hog-tie you to the bed. Don't push it."

It was a warning and a threat so why did a spark of awareness just sizzle down every nerve ending, causing memories of their sweat-slicked bodies sliding against one another to tumble free from the locked box in her head? She swallowed and forcibly shoved those thoughts far from her mind. If she needed a memory of Nathan, she'd just dig out the one where he told her that the idea of having sex with her for the rest of his life was more than he could stomach.

A spasm of pain rippled through her body, giving her an agonizing jolt back to reality. He could not ride in like the hero just because it suited his warped sense of chivalry when he'd been the biggest bastard on the planet two short months ago. Her hands clenched into fists with pent-up rage at the man who'd broken her heart so grievously, and at that moment she didn't care if he was the only body standing between her and a Mexican drug cartel; she didn't want his help or his brand of chivalry. Nathan could choke on his offer of aid and protection, Jaci thought, staring a cold hole through Nathan's back when he turned away from her.

"Screw you, Nathan," she murmured. "I never asked you to save me. If you want to play the hero, play it with someone else. I'm out of here."

She bolted for the door. And she would've made it, too, if Nathan hadn't been bigger, stronger and faster than the feelings of regret and shame that followed on the heels of a drunken binge.

"Damn it, Jaci," he growled, jerking her over his shoulder and slapping her hard on the rear end when she shrieked and began kicking his front and pummeling his back. "I warned you. You're not leaving unless I say so."

"Put me down, you bastard!" Jaci screamed. "I'd rather die than remain stuck in this house with you! I hate you! Do you hear me? I hate you!"

"Yeah, yeah, well, too bad," he shot back. "And if you don't stop wiggling around I swear I'm going to hog-tie you naked!"

"You wouldn't dare!"

"Try me."

She landed a good kick against the hard planes of his stomach and he grunted but otherwise kept his forward pace to the bedroom where he tossed her none too gently onto the bed. She bounced with a shriek and tried to scramble away but Nathan grasped both ankles and yanked her toward him. She kicked and hissed with rage even as tears stung her eyes but she didn't let up. She hoped he got a faceful of flying feet for his trouble.

"Damn it, Jaci!" he roared when she refused to stop. He lunged and straddled her, shocking her with the sudden weight of his body across hers. He captured her flailing arms at the wrists and wrenched them over her head, stretching her so that she couldn't move. Her breath came hard and fast as a long curl of her hair landed across her face, obscuring her vision in her left eye. She angrily blew the hair from her eye and ignored the uncomfortable awareness kindling to life in her body. She would not allow even a spark of attraction to flare, no matter that he remained a stable fixture in her most erotic dreams. It was much too easy to remember how it felt to lie beneath his solid strength, clinging to him as if her life depended on it. She bit down on her tongue and tasted blood. *Remember the pain of his rejection,* she told herself with blunt force. *Remember how you cried for weeks.*

"Are you finished?" he asked in a hard voice. "You need to get a grip. Do you hear me? This is serious. Get that through your damn head. Do you want to die? Is that what this is about? You've just stopped caring about whatever happens to you? That you couldn't really care less if you live or die? Is that why you've been hanging out at sleazy bars and drinking yourself into a stupor every chance you get? What the hell is wrong with you, Jaci?"

She stared up at him, unable to believe what she'd just heard. Had he forgotten how he'd left her? Had he spaced on how he'd ripped her life apart and walked away without caring about the damage? A separate train of thought followed the first as she rapidly blinked away the tears and stared at him with open suspicion. "How do you know I've been going to sleazy bars?" He seemed to realize he'd revealed too much information and faltered for a split second, long enough for Jaci to put two and two together. "Have you been…watching me? Like some creeper stalker?"

His gaze darkened as he scowled. "I'm not a stalker."

"That's what stalkers do, they watch people without the other person's knowledge. Why would you do that?"

He buttoned his lip, clearly unwilling to reveal his reasons, but she didn't care anymore. She couldn't possibly make heads or tails of anything Nathan did or why, nor was she going to start trying. Those days were long gone. "Whatever." She glanced away. "Get the hell off me. My legs are going numb, and if I recall, you were tired of spending any length of time on top of my body, anyway."

Nathan hesitated, his scowl remaining, but he finally climbed off her and she rolled away from him. This time she didn't try to run, but simply stared, waiting for answers.

"I never said I was tired of being on top of you," he said, his mouth compressing to a tight, almost bitter line.

"You said the idea of monogamy with me was more than you could handle. You also said you were bored," Jaci said, trying not to wince at the pain the memory of that day still caused. Holy hell, it felt as if two months had only been two days ago. How pathetic. She'd enabled him to turn her into a weak, pathetic female and she hated him for it. But damn, it still hurt. Did she care? She shouldn't but she did. A part of her needed to know that there was a sliver of humanity inside him that was remorseful for breaking her heart the way that he had. "What's really going on?" she asked. "There's no need to hide the truth from me. We're not a couple. Just tell me so I know what I'm dealing with. Don't you see how it's not fair to drag me from my life without warning and keep me here against my will without at least clueing me in to what's going on?"

"I already told you—"

"You told me the bare minimum, which wasn't an answer at all. Who is after me and why?"

"I'd have to tell you more than you'd want to know. It's better this way," he said, adding quietly. "Trust me."

Had he no idea how impossible his request was? How incapable she was of blithely following him simply because he crooked his finger and patted her on the head with a promise that if she did as she was told like a good girl, everything would be fine? He obviously didn't remember a thing about her personality because never in a million years would she ever be so docile. "The thing about trust is, you have to be willing to be vulnerable with the other person," she said. "And I would never allow myself to be vulnerable with you again."

"You would be willing to jeopardize your life just because you're still pissed off about our breakup? I thought you were smarter than that."

"I thought I was smarter about a lot of things. You, Nathan, proved to me that I'm as stupid as they come."

Nathan heard the ragged pain under her subdued tone and he looked away, unable to hold her stare. If there'd been any other way to keep her safe, he would've done it. Walking away from Jaci had been like tearing off a limb and leaving it behind. And he'd been a bear to be around since then. His personality had never been what one would describe as cuddly, but Jaci had managed to bring out the softer side in him—one he hadn't even known existed—and it'd been that soft, mushy side that had made him realize that if anything ever happened to her because of him, he'd follow her to the grave.

He'd learned long ago that life was filled with pain, but Jaci had been a bright shiny star in a dark universe. How could he possibly allow his feelings for her to put her in jeopardy? The night he'd surprised a man lying in wait in her apartment, Nathan had realized she was no longer safe with him around. The fact that the guy had managed to catch Nathan with a quick uppercut and escape before Nathan could put a bullet through his brain had only served to make Nathan even more on edge. "Are you hungry?" he asked gruffly. "I have food."

"No."

He accepted her answer, even if he knew she was lying through her teeth. Jaci had always loved food. Nathan had relished her softly rounded curves and the way she didn't pretend to pick at a garden salad, protesting how full she was after nibbling a piece of lettuce. No, Jaci had ordered steak and potatoes and then had often eyed the dessert menu. She was the kind of woman who set his blood on fire. "You should eat," he said.

"I said I wasn't hungry. I want to go home."

"It's not safe."

"What about my roommate? He's going to notice if I suddenly go missing."

Nathan scowled at the mention of the man she lived with. He didn't know if there was anything romantic going on but he had his suspicions. What normal red-blooded male could withstand living with a woman like Jaci without making a move of some sort? Unless the man was gay… But Nathan didn't pin much hope on that score, so that made James Public Enemy Number One in Nathan's opinion. "I have a burner phone you can use to let him know you're okay. Tell him you're visiting friends or something but don't let him know where you are." He paused a minute, then couldn't help himself as he asked, "So what's the deal with you two…? Dating?"

"Are you deaf? I said he was my roommate, not my boyfriend, not that it's any of your business. James is a good friend. I needed a place to stay when my *ex-boyfriend* duped me into thinking we were getting a place together and I let my apartment go. Forgive me for not wanting to sleep in my car."

"And he was your only choice? You didn't have a girlfriend you could stay with?"

"Unbelievable! You have some nerve. I'm not even going to dignify that question with a response because you have no right to judge how I solved the problem *you* created. Okay? So butt out."

Nathan backed down, hating that he'd let himself slip like that. On the surface she was right. He shouldn't butt his nose into her personal business, but they weren't your average exes and she'd just have to get used to the idea. "Your safety isn't something I'm going to mess around with. I am going to need to run a background check on this roommate. What's his name?"

"He would never hurt me. We've been friends for years."

"What's his name?" he repeated, not backing down.

"His name is James Cotton."

Nathan committed the name to memory. He'd have a full background check done on the man. If he had so much as an outstanding library book, Nathan would find out. "I'll let you know when you can contact him. Until then, don't bother trying. There's no phone line installed here."

She looked ready to say something childish and petulant—Jaci had always been terrible at hiding her thoughts and feelings—but she buttoned her lips and turned on her heel to return to the bedroom, where she promptly slammed the door.

The message was pretty clear. He wasn't welcome in her space, whether he was saving her damn hide or not.

The knowledge pinched more than a little but he shrugged it off. He wasn't here to start playing house; he was saving her life.

So why was he still staring at that closed door like a starving man stared at a Thanksgiving feast?

Because inside he felt ravenous and out of control, he answered himself as he squeezed his eyes shut.

Shut it down, Isaacs. Stay cool. Now was not the time to start baring his soul and babbling apologies.

Besides…there wasn't anything he could say that would forgive what he'd done.

That'd been the plan.

Chapter 4

"I'll meet you there," Nathan confirmed, ending the call just as Jaci exited the bedroom. He knew she'd heard him so he started talking first. "I want you to stay here while I meet up with a contact who might be able to help me figure out who's after you. Promise me you'll stay put."

"And why should I do that?"

"Because I've already explained that you're safer here than out in the open."

"No, you haven't explained anything. You've *told* me what to do and just expected me to *obey.* That's not the same thing."

Damn redheaded stubborn streak, he wanted to mutter, but instead sent her a hard look, ignoring how his stomach clenched at the sight of her vibrant beauty staring back at him. It didn't seem to matter that she exuded cold distance rather than sweet love like she used to—his heart still quickened dangerously. Emotion got people killed. *Stow that sentimental crap, Isaacs.*

"Jaci, just stay put," he said again, grabbing his gun and tucking it into the back of his waistband beneath his leather jacket. "I won't be gone long. There's plenty of food in the pantry and fridge. The television doesn't work but there should be some books and magazines lying around that might keep you occupied but don't go outside."

Jaci's mutinous expression didn't bode well. The minute he was a mile down the road she was going to bolt, he'd bet his soul on that. He couldn't take the chance. Although it was a risk taking her out into the open, it was a bigger risk to leave her alone and vulnerable. She was operating on pissed-off female ire and brokenhearted steam—she couldn't think clearly to save her life.

"Fine. Get your stuff—you're coming with me. But—" he fixed her with a hard stare hoping she caught his drift "—if you so much as take one single step away from my side or do one single thing that puts your life in more danger, I swear to God, I will make you regret it. Don't push me on this. Am I clear?" This was no idle threat. He'd do whatever it took to keep her safe, even if it meant humiliating her. "Am I clear?" he asked, his tone sharp. At her slow nod and quick disappearance into the bedroom he knew he'd gotten his point across. If there was one thing Jaci needed to remember about him it was that he never took unnecessary chances, particularly with the lives of the ones he loved the most.

Jaci reappeared fully dressed and quickly came down the stairs. "Where we going?" she asked. "Or am I not supposed to know?"

"I've got a friend on the inside of the organization I work for. We're going to meet him and see if we can figure out what the hell's going on."

Jaci nodded, surprising him with her easy acceptance. Either she was privately formulating an escape plan or she was actually starting to trust him. Ha. Yeah, nothing was that easy. Chances were she was simply pretending to acquiesce when in truth she was going to sprint like a rabbit in a clearing the minute she was able.

Jaci climbed into the big four-wheel-drive truck required to reach this secluded location deep in the mountains and while she may not have said anything, he could see the appreciation for the vehicle in her eyes. "What happened to the Mustang?" she asked, buckling up. "I thought that car was your baby."

"It is. And that's why it's still parked safely in a garage. There's no way the Mustang would've made it up the roads in this area." He cast her a sideways glance. "Besides, I thought you liked big trucks."

"I used to like a lot of things."

He didn't buy her cool answer but didn't see the value in pushing. "It gets the job done," he said, putting the truck into gear and rumbling down the pocked and rutted service road. "Have you noticed anything unusual happening lately?"

"Such as?"

"Have you felt as if someone was watching you, or maybe sensed that you were being followed?" he asked.

"No, of course not." Jaci gasped as the truck hit a particularly deep rut and sent her bouncing in her seat. She quickly grasped the handle above the door and held on for dear life. "If I'd noticed any of those things I would've called the police. I'm not stupid. My life has been normal. I go to work, go to the gym, go to the grocery store and do all of those normal things that normal people do. I don't know what the hell is going on and why I'm in the middle of it. Of course, *you* seem to have some inkling as to why this is going on but you won't tell me so I am left to wonder why my life is imploding for no particular reason."

"If I knew why this was happening, I'd already have taken care of the situation," he corrected her tersely, irritated by her comment. As if he were withholding information simply to mess with her. "C'mon, Jase… you're smarter than that."

"Well, that remains to be seen," she muttered. "Besides, if someone was trying to kill me why did they kill Sonia instead?"

"She was a witness. No loose ends. If you recall, you were seconds away from sharing the same fate as your friend."

He hated to be so blunt but he didn't see the value in sugarcoating the truth, as much as he could tell her, anyway. "Have you been dating?" he asked, steeling himself for her answer. It was important information, he told himself, not for personal reasons but because he needed to eliminate suspects. Well, it was a plausible justification, but when Jaci shrugged and admitted to a few dates his blood percolated. "Who? I need names."

She shot him a dark look. "No one serious. I wasn't interested in getting in a serious relationship after what'd happened with you and me. But Sonia convinced me that I couldn't live like a hermit and I thought the best way to get over you would be to see other people."

"Did it work?" Why the hell did he ask that? "Never mind. I shouldn't have asked. It doesn't matter. Tell me about your dates. I need to run them through a background check."

She scowled. "They were normal people. Bankers, a doctor, I think a lawyer or two, I don't know. But they sure as hell weren't spies. And none of them worked for the government in any capacity."

"Jaci, people lie. And you are a very trusting person so your doctors and lawyers, unless you do a full background check on them, may not have been who they said they were. I told you I worked for the FBI. You never thought to look any deeper."

He detested to throw in her face how he'd duped her but the pain was necessary to get through her head that people were unscrupulous at best, and dangerous at their worst. Jaci looked away and remained quiet for a long moment. Finally she said, "I met them through an online dating service. If I can get to a computer I can log on to my site and show you who I was matched up with. Would that help?"

Nathan did a double take. "An online dating service? Why would you go through one of those sites? It's not like you couldn't find a date on your own. Don't you know those places are ripe for liars? Why would you take such a risk?"

"You don't get to criticize how I lead my life after you left me. For your information, online dating is something that everybody does. It's not just for the sad, lonely, pathetic losers that you're making it sound like. Most people have careers and don't have time to hang out in bars to meet someone. And frankly, why would I want to meet someone to build a life with in a bar?" She didn't have to remind him that they'd met in a bar. He remembered quite clearly. He also caught her subtle dig. "Besides, I wasn't looking for Mr. Right. I was just looking for someone to spend a little time with."

"So you were just taking home random guys for sex?"

Jaci lifted her chin. "Yes, that's right. I have needs, too. Are you saying that when we broke up you became celibate?"

How did they end up talking about their sex lives? He hated knowing that Jaci had been with other men after their breakup, but what had he expected? Hell, he'd tried to tell himself that letting her go was a noble gesture on his part so that she could meet someone normal and get married and have a family. He couldn't have it both ways—let her go, plus expect her to live like a nun.

"Of course not," he said, answering her question. "I saw other people," he lied. Nathan didn't want to admit to her that when he'd become accustomed to steak, the prospect of hamburger simply hadn't appealed. "My point is, there's a possibility that someone you dated may be trying to kill you. I can't discount the possibility. And as uncomfortable as it may be for the both of us to talk about the people who came after us I can't simply ignore the possible lead just because it hurts to talk about it."

"Why would it hurt you? You were the one who left me, remember?"

"Yes, Jaci, I remember." He gritted his teeth, pausing a moment to withstand the surge of defensive anger that followed her pointed reminder. "Very clearly. And leaving you hurt like a son of a bitch."

"I don't believe you," she shot back heatedly. "You can't rewrite history just because you suddenly don't like the part you played. I was in love with you. I wanted to get married and have kids and build a life together. I thought we were on the same page but you corrected my assumptions, didn't you? So, no, I don't believe you when you say that it hurt you to leave me. And I find it insulting that you would even try to make me believe that lie."

What could he say? He understood where she was coming from. If the shoe had been on the other foot—if she had done to him what he had done to her—

there was nothing that she would've been able to say to change his mind. Would it help if he tried to apologize? She deserved at least that but he didn't know how to formulate the words. "Jaci…I—" he began, but she shut him down quickly.

"Don't. Whatever you have to say, I don't want to hear. I just want to put all of this behind me and forget I ever met you. I was close to having closure when you burst back into my life. I don't want to do this anymore. I don't want to cry, I don't want to wonder, I don't want to think of what might've been. I just want to be free of you."

Oh, God, that hurt. Nathan's jaw tightened as he willed the pain away. She'd said her piece and he had to respect her for it. He understood her need for closure. And if that's what she wanted from him, he'd give it to her. As soon as he knew she was safe, he would walk away and never bother her again. But until then, until he knew there was no one who wanted her dead, he would stick to her like glue. Anyone who wanted to hurt Jaci would have to go through him first. And he was one hell of a moving target with an even deadlier aim.

Damn him. How dare he try to rewrite history as if he hadn't set in motion everything that had taken place. He wasn't allowed to be hurt or express pain over their breakup because he was the one who had shattered her heart into a million pieces. He didn't get the option of sharing his regret. And if that seemed unfair, so be it. She didn't care.

She blinked back tears. No, she wouldn't cry. She refused to be that weak, weeping woman who fell apart at the slightest sign of a crisis. She was stronger than that. At least she wanted to be. She had to be strong for Sonia. Her best friend had died for being in the wrong place at the wrong time. If Nathan thought he could figure out who was after her, then she had to let him try. But first, she needed a few things. "We need to stop by my apartment. I'm not going on the run wearing nothing but club clothes that smell like stale cigarettes and alcohol." *Not to mention blood splatter,* Jaci thought, fighting the rise of nausea and grief. "And I want to know what happened to my friend. I don't care who you have to call or what you have to do but I need answers. I need to know that my best friend is being taken care of." Tears stung her eyes. "Do you understand? I need to know that Sonia was properly put to rest."

Nathan didn't look happy with her request but he seemed to understand her need for closure. "If you promise to stick to my side, as in no running off doing anything crazy or reckless, I'll tell you what I know of what happened after we left the scene."

She made a face. "You're negotiating?"

"I'm securing your cooperation. Make your choice."

She crossed her arms. "Fine. I agree to stick to your side like glue if you tell me what happened after you forced me to leave my best friend lying in a pool of her own blood," she spat, hating him.

He scowled. "You mean after I saved your pretty head from sporting the same wound, which is what would've happened if we had stuck around a minute longer," he corrected her sharply and she blinked back angry tears.

Why couldn't someone else have been her savior? Anyone but him! She knew she owed him her life but she was fairly choking on the gratitude she was supposed to feel.

But then a fleeting expression of remorse passed over his features as he added, "Jaci…if I could have saved your friend, I would have." And she knew she was being harsh.

She looked away, acknowledging. "I know," she whispered but she could almost taste the bitterness in her tone. "I can't believe she's gone. She always had my back. Always. No matter what. She agreed to walk down that alley because I didn't want anyone to see me throw up. She was the best friend a girl could ever want."

He sighed. "I made some calls and your friend's murder is currently on the desk of a detective who is known for closing cases. The nature of the case is enough to stir interest—young woman with no criminal record with a single bullet wound to the head—because it's not as if she were connected to any kind of criminal element that might've put her there. Not to mention, the second body of the thug, which won't make sense at all."

"So, won't the investigation lead to your organization at some point?"

"No. As far as the government is concerned, we don't exist. The investigation will fall short of leads and eventually get thrown into the cold case file."

Jaci stared, not happy with his explanation. "Sonia's family deserves some kind of closure. Not knowing why their daughter died will kill them."

"I'm sorry. I can't do anything about that."

"I don't believe you."

He held her accusatory stare. "In this, I have no reason to lie. If there was something I could do, I would. If it helps any, Sonia's death was quick. She felt no pain."

"It doesn't," she snapped, wiping at the tears that escaped to roll down her cheeks. "Nothing helps."

"I know."

"Do you?" Jaci's shoulders bowed as another wave of pain rocked her body as Nathan watched. He didn't have the right to gather her into his arms and hold her tightly, murmuring words of comfort against her hair, but for one second she wished he would ignore all that and just pull her to him. Jaci wiped away her tears, drawing a halting breath. "Thank you for at least making the call to find out," she said grudgingly, but then added, "When this is all over, I will explain to Sonia's parents what really happened. I won't let them suffer for the rest of their days. It's bad enough they lost their daughter." Nathan opened his mouth, looking intent on shutting her down, but he let it ride. Some of the tension left her shoulders and she no longer felt as if someone's hands were around her throat. She rolled her neck, ready to focus and said, "At some point you're going to have to level with me. I have to know what's going on."

"When I feel it's safe to share more information I will."

She accepted his answer. She supposed that was the best she could get at the moment. Everything felt surreal. Was she really sitting in the passenger side of Nathan's truck, running for her life? Twenty-four hours ago she'd been a normal girl, someone who dreamed of a home and family. Someone who dreamed of meeting the one person who would love her above all else.

After Nathan, she wasn't sure that person existed. Well, that wasn't entirely true. She'd been so positive that Nathan had been The One for her. She hadn't wanted anyone else. She hadn't been open to finding a replacement, either. All of the blind dates, endless dinners and soulless quickies that'd only satisfied a physical need but hadn't come close to satisfying the emotional void that existed in her heart—they'd all been her desperate attempt to erase the one person who had done so much damage.

And now he was here again. Saving her life, *supposedly*. How did she know that he wasn't simply a psycho who enjoyed playing with her mind and heart? There were people like that out there; she'd watched an episode of *Law and Order* where this guy pretended to be someone he wasn't simply because he got off messing with other people's lives.

Oh, God. Now she was considering conspiracy theories. Maybe she just needed food so she could start thinking rationally again. "I'm starving," she announced. "Is food on your agenda today?"

"There was food back at the cabin."

She fought the urge to stick her tongue out at him.

He sighed. "Yeah, we can pick up some food."

Good. Apparently she didn't need to remind him how peckish she became when her blood sugar plummeted. She thanked him with the tiniest pinch of gratitude necessary for his concession and returned her gaze to the dense forest surrounding them. He'd been right; she would've been lost and tumbling into a ravine if she'd struck out on her own. Damn. She hated how directionally challenged she was. Right about now she was wishing she'd paid more attention in school.

Silence filled the cab as neither seemed interested in attempting small talk. Not that she would've been capable of rambling on about nothing in particular. Her mind was a fractured landscape as her thoughts bounced from one thought to the other. Jaci didn't know what was safe to think about, as each memory seemed suspect, or worse, painful.

Maybe she should've asked Nathan to drug her again. Blissful oblivion might've been a better option than this agonizing reality. She closed her eyes.

Please let this be over soon.

Chapter 5

"Hey man, what's going on? It's like the whole world's been turned upside down and suddenly you're the main characters in an *Alias* episode."

Nathan edged past his friend George, not interested in having this conversation in the hallway. "What have you heard?" he asked, once George, a weapons expert who dabbled in conspiracy theories, closed the door and began the laborious process of flipping the intricate locking system he had in place. "What kind of chatter is there?"

George shook his head as he flopped into his swiveling chair that looked a lot like a throne encased in black leather, and immediately appeared distressed. "Something's going down, man. Something big. When you told me to start nosing around I said, yeah, hey man, that's cool. I don't mind poking my nose where it don't belong. But I think I've uncovered some serious shit. I'm talking movie-plot, James Cameron–grade, Hollywood-type espionage. *Bourne-Identity*—"

"I get the point," Nathan interrupted, moving George along. "What'd you find?"

"You know that kill order you intercepted for your lady…"

"I'm not his lady," Jaci corrected George stiffly, shooting Nathan a dark look. "We aren't together. Haven't been for two months."

"Right. Whatever. Anyway, the kill order for your ex, well, it was supposed to go deeper than that."

"What do you mean?" Jaci asked before Nathan could. "Deeper than what?"

"And that's the question, isn't it?" George replied with cryptic flair. He startled Jaci when he leaned forward suddenly but then eyed Nathan. "Whose cereal have you pissed in lately, 'cause this job was a twofer."

"What are you talking about?" Nathan asked. "I saw the kill order—it was only for Jaci."

"No, you saw the dummy order. The real order was a murder-suicide twofer. So, that makes me wonder, who the hell did you cheese off that they wanted you out of the way, and taking the blame for some heinous crime?"

"Good question," Nathan agreed with a scowl. "Who indeed?"

"Are you telling me that someone in your own organization wants not only me, but you dead, too?" The incredulity in Jaci's voice mirrored how Nathan felt, as well. The situation had soured more quickly than milk left out overnight in the heat of summer. "This is just fabulous. So, now, I'm not the only one with a price on my head for reasons unknown but the man who is supposed to protect me is also wanted dead by the very people who sign his paycheck. Fabulous. We're so screwed."

"Shut it down a minute, Jase," Nathan warned, needing a minute to think things through. He looked to George. "Where did you find the real order?"

"I cashed in a few favors. I know a guy who knows a guy who heard some chatter in certain circles," George answered, clearly proud of himself for digging up such a find. "But here's the thing—my skills weren't able to uncover where the order originated. Whoever created the order must be someone important because no one's naming names if they want to live to see tomorrow. I know stuff like this happens in the movies, but in real life? Makes me glad I don't trust no one and I'm armed to the teeth."

"Focus, George," Nathan muttered, thinking hard. "You might want to lay low for a while. You might be in danger, too, for poking around. Whoever buried this order isn't going to be pleased that someone uncovered their dirty laundry. And if they have the skills to bury this order that deep, don't you think they know how to follow your trail right to your padlocked door?"

George sobered and sat straighter, his gaze suddenly serious. "I didn't think of that. Aw, man, I don't want to move. Do you know how hard it was to find this apartment in a rent-controlled area?"

"George, you live in a run-down apartment building that was built in the '50s. Let's get real."

"Yeah, but my neighbors don't bug me and they mind their own business. You can't put a price on that."

"You can't put a price on breathing, either," Nathan pointed out dryly.

"Good point. I'll keep my eyes open."

"Anything else I should know?"

"Just that you might very well be screwed," George admitted with a chagrined expression. "That sucks, dude. I wish I had better news. So what's your plan? Leaving the country?"

"Leave the country?" Jaci gasped. "I can't leave the country. I have a life here in *this* country. I have a job…I have…well, reasons to stick around like plans for the future and stuff like that."

"Good luck with that," George retorted. "The guy they sent after you? There's more where he came from."

"Who the hell do you work for?" Jaci stared in horror at Nathan. "The Mafia?"

"Worse," he answered. "The government." He dug into his pocket and pulled a few hundreds free and tossed them to George. "For your trouble. You didn't see us and you haven't heard from me, either."

"No problemo, *mi amigo,*" George said, scooping up the cash. "Seriously though, dude. Watch your back. Someone's gunning for you big time."

"Thanks."

George let them out and then as the locks slid back into place, Nathan and Jaci booked it for the truck. He'd been uncomfortable being out in the open before, but now he felt downright suicidal walking around in the light of day knowing a sniper could have them in his sights at any minute.

Hell, the situation just went from bad to worse.

Jaci was going to freak.

"A framed murder-suicide? Does that actually happen in real life? I mean, that's a movie plot, not something that happens to real people who live normal lives with regular jobs like me. I've never even fudged my taxes before. Lots of people do it but not me—I'm terrified of being audited so I walk the line and give away gobs of potential write-offs because I don't want to take the chance and now I have a killer, sanctioned by the freaking government, who wants me dead. Am I the only one who finds this remotely crazy to even consider as a possibility?"

Nathan shot her a look but otherwise didn't respond to her frantic rambling, which only spurred her to ramble more as her panic hit a crescendo.

"What are we supposed to do? Pack up our lives and go on the run, changing our names every few months, living in rat-infested apartments so we can go off the grid? I don't want to live like that. I can't live like that. I can barely remember my social security number, much less a new identity every few months. I'd trip up and inadvertently give out the wrong information and probably get us killed! Oh, God. We're living on borrowed time, aren't we? Unbelievable. I was a good girl! I was honest and kind and compassionate. I donated to animal shelters and even adopted a village in Kenya because I read that five dollars a day could provide clean drinking water for an entire village and now…? I'm being hunted like a dog! Whatever happened to good karma? Surely I've banked a little by now!"

"Jaci!"

"What?"

"Take a deep breath and shut up for a second. I will not let anything happen to you. I promise," Nathan assured her, gripping her chin and forcing her to look at him. If she hadn't been bordering on a nervous breakdown, she would've slapped his hand away, but as it was she was trembling on the edge and needed someone to take charge and tell her it was going to be all right even if it was total crap. "I'm going to figure out what the hell is going on and I'm going to stop whoever is trying to kill us both. In the meantime, we're going to hole up and lay low. Okay?"

She jerked a short nod as her eyes filled. "I don't want to die," she whispered.

"I don't want to die, either," he said, his mouth twisting in a subtle grin that did something undesirable to her insides. "Who says we never had anything in common?"

She wiped at her eyes. "Not funny."

"Too soon?"

"Way too soon." She pulled away. "So I'm guessing a trip to my apartment is out of the question."

"It's the first place they'll expect you to go. Sorry. You'll have to make do with what we can find at the cabin."

"Fine." She glanced down at her dirty skirt. "I can always hand wash what I'm wearing."

Nathan eyed her skirt with open distaste and she bristled just a little. "You don't have to look at me if I'm so offensive to your sensibilities." She winced privately at the memory of his mocking her when he'd broken her heart. He'd had plenty to say about her long, coltlike legs. For the first time ever, he'd made her feel as if having long legs wasn't something to be desired. She pulled at her skirt, trying to cover herself better.

"You're not offending me," he admitted, but his gaze said otherwise as it seemed he couldn't bear to let his stare drift to her bare legs.

"Good, because I don't really care what you think anyway," she snapped before she could help herself. *Okay, take a deep breath.* Like it or not, Nathan was all that stood between her and some crazy person's agenda, which included her death. "I'm sorry," she amended. "My nerves are a bit jangled and I'm not myself. I'm not going to lie and say that I don't have some unresolved issues about the way we broke up but I know that's not important right now. I'm trying desperately to hold on to the big picture, but let's just say that I'm not as emotionally mature as I'd like to be under the circumstances."

"No need to apologize," he said gruffly. "I get it."

A man of many words. She bit her tongue to keep from snapping again. Here she was trying to be the bigger person and he was uttering small quips and sound bites. Would it kill him to express a deeper thought? Particularly when they were facing mortal peril? What if this was their last possible chance to share their feelings?

What feelings? A nasty voice reminded her. Nathan Isaacs wasn't human. She settled her thoughts firmly before she completely lost control of her mouth again. Neither of them were overjoyed at being in forced proximity but both enjoyed breathing so they'd just have to make the best of things. She could handle being around Nathan for a short time, right? She'd just have to wrap her brain around the fact that he was her protector, not her ex-lover who broke her spirit and heart in one fell swoop.

And she'd also have to ignore the memories of what it felt like to be beneath all that straining muscle, clutching at each other like love-drunk monkeys.

Yeah, piece of cake.

Chapter 6

Nathan didn't trust a silent woman—particularly one who had a history of being chatty. They'd returned to the cabin and Jaci had started to search for alternate clothing but the subtle frown etched on her brow told him her thoughts were elsewhere. Should he try and talk to her? Did she need to vent or something? The thing about being an assassin was that no one had ever accused him of being warm and sensitive. He pulled triggers for a living; he didn't do touchy-feely unless it was of the naked variety.

Yet he felt compelled to do something that might help Jaci get through this terrible predicament. "Do you want to talk?" he ventured, almost cringing.

"No."

Thank God. No, wait. "Jaci, I know this is a stressful thing but we're going to be all right."

"Please don't patronize me," she said in exasperation as she dropped an ugly oversize sweater that looked like a reject from the '70s. "I know we're in serious trouble. I'm trying to deal with it the best way that I can and in the meantime, I'm trying to find clothing that doesn't look like something used as a costume for a community-theater melodrama. Who lived here? There's not a single article of clothing that isn't terribly dated or four times too big."

"I don't know. I bought it a long time ago when I thought I'd need a safe house or a place to decompress. I've only been here a few times over the years, mostly between missions. The clothes I picked up at the local thrift store to make it look as if someone lives here. If someone were to peek through the windows, they'd see a lived-in place, which is a deterrent to anyone who might want to try and squat in a vacant house."

"There are no other human beings on this mountain. The only squatters you need to worry about are the bears and I don't think they're going to care if there are clothes in the closet." She sighed and surveyed the pile of rejects. "I'm sorry but there's nothing here that even fits. If we don't find a way to get some clothes, I'm going to end up running around in my bra and panties the whole time."

His mind blanked at the idea and he nearly groaned out loud. Good God. He couldn't let that happen. If he saw Jaci in nothing but her skivvies, he was likely to throw her down and bury himself inside that gorgeous body of hers—definitely a bad idea. He must have grimaced for Jaci sent him a hard scowl as she said, "Don't worry. I'll drape myself in a plastic tarp before I subject your poor eyeballs to my naked body. I do recall how disgusted you were with what I have to offer."

Ah, hell. If only she knew the truth. "I don't need distractions," he said instead, which only made her angrier and he cursed himself for being a clumsy clod when it came to saying the right thing. She stiffened and lifted her chin, her eyes glittering, and he knew she was about to tear him a new one so he cut her off before she could begin. "Jaci, before you get started… I'm going to say this and then leave it be. If you start prancing around in nothing but your skin, I can't promise that I will keep my hands to myself. It's been a long time since I've had a woman beneath me and you'll do just fine. You getting me?"

She rolled her eyes. "So you're saying that you're desperate enough to find me attractive? Gee, thanks."

Hell, that's not what he meant at all. He dreamed of holding Jaci in his arms again. He got hard just thinking of the times he'd been lucky enough to have had the privilege of peeling her clothes from her lush body. But he couldn't keep her safe if he didn't keep his head on a swivel and that trumped his baser needs. "Yeah, that's what I'm saying."

"You're a jerk."

"Yeah, well, I've been called worse."

"If my life weren't in danger and you weren't the

one person watching out for me, I'd push you in front of a bus."

Nathan watched as she turned on her heel and ran to the bedroom, slamming the door behind her. He squeezed his eyes shut and rubbed his temples as a tension headache threatened to burst his brain. How was he going to survive being cooped up with that woman for longer than a day or two? Too bad the Geneva Conventions didn't have a clause about forcing former lovers into close proximity for extended periods of time.

Particularly if the female is a fiery, temperamental redhead with a body that makes a man's teeth clench and his pants tight.

Surely that had to be inhumane.

Jerk. Jerk. Jerk.

That was Nathan Isaacs's middle name. In fact, it was probably typed on his birth certificate. She wasn't ugly or hard on the eyes. Plenty of men had assured her that she was pretty, not that she'd gone looking for compliments—well, maybe just a little. She could admit that her self-esteem had taken a beating after Nathan had dumped her.

And now he was messing with her again.

As if she'd even invite him into her bed again after how he'd treated her. Not a chance. The idea of allowing Nathan to touch even one inch of her skin made her want to retch. If the earth depended on her having a rematch of cuddle time with Nathan, the human race would go extinct because he didn't deserve to sniff her hair much less rub up against her in any way.

But if she was so abhorrent to him, why did his eyes glaze over at the thought of her running around naked? She was a little rusty in interpreting Nathan's expressions but she could've sworn she'd seen lust reflecting in his stare. But that couldn't be right because when they'd broken up, he'd plainly stated he was no longer attracted to her. Had he lied? Why would he? Was she grasping at straws in the hopes of salvaging some shred of dignity or pride? Probably. She flopped down on the bed and stared at the ceiling. Exhaustion was setting in. Her brain was scrambled and she was clearly not operating on all four cylinders because if she were, she wouldn't be trying to make sense out of the actions of a man she'd never truly known. Her eyelids dragged and she allowed them to close. Sleep was good. Maybe when she woke up, things would be clearer.

Maybe when she woke up she'd discover that none of this had happened. She'd open her eyes and find herself back at her apartment, back to her regular life where no one was trying to kill her and her best friend Sonia was texting her to not forget the tortilla chips and salsa for Margarita Girls' Night In.

Maybe.

Hopefully.

Nathan opened his laptop and attached his remote Hotspot to enable the internet connection. Within seconds his email popped up with an urgent message from his director, Tom Wyatt. The text was simple. Worried. Come talk.

Nathan knew he could trust Tom but he didn't want to put anyone else at risk until he knew what he was dealing with. He typed a quick reply, Will be in touch, and hit Send. He needed more information before he went to Tom with evidence that someone was dirty inside their tight-knit department. The problem? Nathan didn't know where to start.

How was he supposed to figure out who had it out for him if he didn't know where to start looking? Perhaps the dead guy could lend a clue. It had been dark so getting a good look at his mug had been impossible but Nathan had a few contacts he could tap in the coroner's office for an ID. He couldn't risk a phone call—he didn't know how secure the lines were—so that meant he'd have to make a trip back down the mountain to the coroner's office. He hated the idea of venturing into the open again but his back was up against the wall. Besides, he supposed he couldn't put off another trip for too much longer. Otherwise he ran the risk of Jaci prancing around in nothing but her skin and while he might've talked a good game, it wouldn't take much to tear apart his defenses when it came to seeing Jaci naked.

As if on cue, an erection began to grow behind his zipper. Just the idea of seeing Jaci in her birthday suit was enough to get his motor running. No! He was not about to mess with Jaci like that. He'd broken her heart on purpose and he wasn't going to negate all that heartache just to get his rocks off.

He ought to clear the air with Jaci, just so there weren't hard feelings between them—or at the very least, no *new* hard feelings—but as he headed toward the bedroom, he suffered the distinct feeling that he was about to enter the lion's den.

However, as he pushed the door open slowly, he was surprised to see Jaci crashed out, sleeping hard. He didn't blame her. Emotional fatigue was tough to run from. Grief, confusion and adrenaline made for a tumultuous emotional cocktail and eventually, the body just shut down to catch up. Jaci was sprawled across the bed, her position catching him in a tight spot between longing and too many memories.

"You're ticklish," Jaci said with a surprised giggle as a memory popped loose from his mental cache. They'd spent the afternoon in bed at a small bed-and-breakfast he'd found on the northern coast. There'd been no phone, no cable and no internet access—and it had been heaven. The weekend had been filled with sex, food and more sex with a shower or two thrown in to rinse off their activities so they could start fresh. And Jaci had discovered, quite by accident, his tickle spot right below his rib cage.

"No tickling," he'd said with mock seriousness as he flipped her onto her back. "Otherwise, I'll have to reciprocate and I know you're ticklish all over."

"I can't help that my skin is sensitive," she'd said

with a playful grin. "Every little touch is like a sensory smorgasbord."

"Hmm… A smorgasbord… An all-you-can-eat buffet with Jaci on the menu… Sounds like my kind of place," he had murmured as he dipped lower to kiss the soft skin of her belly. The skin, fair and unblemished, was unlike any he'd ever seen. Her legs went on for miles and her breasts were full and high, almost more perfect than any natural breasts he'd ever seen. He had moved a little lower, lightly grazing the sensitive skin above her feminine folds with the stubble on his chin. "How about here?" She'd squealed in response and he'd grinned. "Or here?" He'd traveled to her inner thigh and sucked a tiny spot of flesh into his mouth. She had nearly rocketed off the bed, gasping.

"I give! I give! No more," she had begged but Nathan had begun to see the allure of tickling and wanted to tease her just a bit more. He'd spent the next forty-five minutes discovering all the places that made Jaci tremble and moan.

He exhaled softly and shook off the memory. He hated knowing that other men had touched her intimately since they'd broken up. Intellectually he'd known that a woman as striking as Jaci wouldn't stay lonely long but emotionally it tore him up to know that other men had been with her.

God, he missed her. He couldn't admit it out loud but he could admit it in the privacy of his mind. He missed everything about her. Hell, he even missed the sound of her off-key notes bouncing off the shower walls as she murdered every popular song on the radio. But mostly he missed the quiet evenings alone where they did their own thing but still managed to feel connected. It'd been in those moments when he'd felt normal—as if they were simply like any couple on the block who hosted backyard barbecues and pool parties with friends and argued about where to put the ugly art she seemed to enjoy or the tacky beer signs he favored. What a cruel joke fate had pulled on them both.

Nathan pushed away from the door and closed it behind him. He'd left Jaci to keep her safe. Even if it cost him his life, he'd make sure that no harm ever came to her. Whether she wanted it or not, that was his promise to her.

Chapter 7

"Where are we going again?" Jaci asked, hurrying after Nathan in her disguise. A cheap blond wig covered her natural brilliant red and she'd finally managed to find some clothes that covered her body, though they were hardly the height of fashion. "And where did you find these clothes? They're nearly as bad as the ones at the cabin," she grumbled.

"Thrift store," he answered, crossing the street quickly. "And we're going to talk with a friend of mine who works at the coroner's office."

"Coroner? As in, where they keep dead people?" Jaci asked with a worried expression. "Why are we going there?"

"Because she might be able to help me identify the

man who tried to kill you. I don't have access to my work computer right now and I don't trust going into the office now that I know someone within my department is out to kill me. So, it's old-school detective time."

"Were you ever a detective?"

"No."

"Then how would you know how a detective operates?"

"I've watched a few *Law and Order* episodes," he said, shooting her a mildly playful look that caused her to blush. *Law and Order* was one of her favorite shows and one she'd always tried getting him to watch with her. He'd succumbed to her wishes a few times in exchange for sexual favors. It'd been a fun game for them both. She got snuggle time in front of the television and he got…well, he got what he wanted.

They entered through the back door and descended four flights of stairs before popping out at the basement. Jaci shivered and muttered, "Aren't morgues scary enough? Why do they have to put them in basements, too? It's damn creepy down here. I feel like I could get murdered right now."

He smiled briefly and knocked softly at the first door at the end of the hall. The metal door opened and Mina, a short, curvaceous woman with a penchant for oddities and a faint European accent, smiled when she saw Nathan but openly ignored Jaci. "It's about time you showed your mug around here, you sexy piece of meat. Get in here," she said, grabbing Nathan and practically dragging him into her inner sanctum.

Jaci cleared her throat meaningfully and Mina flicked an irritated look her way. "Why'd you bring a chaperone? Afraid I'll change your life and ruin you for other women?" Mina teased, causing Nathan to choke back a grin. Good God, if he were of a mind, Mina probably would ruin him—and leave lasting scars. "What can I do you for? It's not very often I get such handsome visitors."

"Mina, I have to warn you, I'm in some trouble. Seems someone wants my head and they're not being very conservative in their efforts."

"I always figured I'd find you on my slab one of these days. Frankly, I'm surprised you've managed to stay alive this long. Who wants you dead?"

"We don't know," Jaci interjected herself into the conversation, sending Nathan a dark look for not introducing her. She held out her hand. "I'm Jaci, his ex-girlfriend. And you are?"

"Mina Harlan. Ex-girlfriend?" She looked to Nathan. "You crafty bastard. You never told me you had a girl, ex or otherwise." Nathan shifted on the balls of his feet, uncomfortable with the conversation. He'd never slept with Mina—he rarely mixed business with pleasure—but Mina had never been quiet about her designs on getting him into her bed. Before Jaci, Nathan might've been tempted but at his core, he was a one-woman kind of man.

Mina sighed and shrugged. "Well, we never would've

suited long-term but we might have made one helluva dent in the mattress. Anyway, you have questions about the ugly gorilla that came across my slab a few days ago, right?"

"Yes," Nathan answered, relieved to return the conversation to safer ground. "What do you know about him?"

"I know that he had liver damage, likely from alcohol abuse, and that his arteries were clogged. If you hadn't killed him, his heart would've in a few years. The poor sap was a walking heart attack."

"Did you get a positive ID from his prints?"

"That's where it gets interesting," she said, going to her desk to pull her notes. "His prints don't belong to him. According to his prints, his name is Olaf Girgich and he died thirty years ago. Your thug is a ghost."

"How is that possible?" Jaci asked.

"His records were switched with Olaf Girgich's," Nathan answered grimly. "Chances are, whoever this man was, he's been off the grid for quite some time. Either he's been working as someone's hired killer for a while or someone managed to make him disappear to hide the trail. Either scenario has merit."

"I'm no Pollyanna but I've got to admit that all this subterfuge and smoke-and-mirrors stuff is really freaking me out. What branch of the government do you work for?" Jaci asked.

"A secret one," Nathan answered.

She scowled and crossed her arms. "You mean the kind that erases people's identities?"

"Yeah." Nathan looked to Mina who appeared amused by their little interchange and gestured. "Is there anything else you can tell us about 'Olaf'?"

Mina smiled but shook her head. "Sorry, that's about where my expertise ends. However, I don't know if this is useful or not but I can tell you that his body was identified by someone other than a family member."

"Who?"

"His body was identified by a man named Derek Nichols and before you ask, yes, I have a contact number for him," Mina said. "Chances are the phone number is bogus but the man has to be buried somewhere legally and that requires a working contact name and number. The man was released to the Burns Mortuary downtown. You might find someone there who knows a bit more about our mysterious 'Olaf.'"

"Good work, Mina."

"Now we're going to a mortuary? What is this, the Halloween tour? Maybe we could drop by a cemetery on our way to round out our day of creepy experiences," Jaci said with a shudder.

"Dead people aren't creepy—they can't hurt you. It's the live ones I worry about. Some human beings are messed up folk. Trust me on that one," Mina said. "Now get out of here before I'm seen talking to you and end up on my own slab."

"I owe you one, Mina," Nathan promised as he and Jaci exited the room and headed for the stairwell.

"Do we really need to go to a mortuary?" Jaci asked.

"Unless you know someone who knows their way

around computers and can hack into the mortuary's business files, then yes, we need to make a trip to the mortuary." At Jaci's sudden reflective pause, he raised an eyebrow and asked, "Do you know someone who can hack into computer files without being detected?"

"Maybe," she hedged, chewing her lip. "But you're not going to like him."

"Him? Him who?"

"My roommate, James. His nickname is Ghost because he can get in and out of any computer program or system without being seen. He's a bit of an obnoxious hacker in his free time."

Nathan's gaze narrowed. "What does he do for a living?"

"He blogs."

"Blogs? That's a job?"

Jaci scowled. "Yes, it's a job and a well-paying one if you know what you're doing." Nathan made a sound of disbelief and she said, "Listen, he might be our best bet at finding the information you're looking for. You dragged me to a morgue to check out a lead, the least you can do is try and test out my source. I can ask Ghost to access their computer files and see what information they logged. It will save us the trip and besides, the mortuary wouldn't volunteer that information without a warrant and it's not as if you can actually legally procure that right now. So, backdoor channels are our only option."

"You're right," Nathan admitted though not happy about it. "But we're not going to your apartment. He'll have to log on somewhere other than his ISP. Does he have a laptop?" She nodded. "Good," he said. "I'll give you a burner phone to call him and set it up. We need to meet somewhere semiprivate yet public at the same time. Safety in numbers and obscurity."

"How about the public library? It's huge but they have areas for private computer use. In fact, there's one computer bay that's a closed room for people who use Dragon for dictation and can't have outside noise messing it up."

"That'll work," he said, impressed.

"Good," she said, rubbing her stomach and looking around. "In the meantime, we need to find some food. I'm starved."

Jaci and the dictates of her raging appetite. "There's a taco truck around the corner. We'll grab something there and then meet your roommate."

Jaci agreed and eagerly followed him. He forcibly shoved away the warm and comfortable feeling of being around Jaci. This was temporary and if anything, this recent situation had only reinforced his previous belief that being around him put Jaci in danger.

A few blocks up he ducked into a Chinese restaurant and reemerged with a packaged phone, gesturing for Jaci to keep moving as he ripped the packaging open and powered it up.

"I can understand kung pao chicken being on the menu but disposable phones?" she asked.

"The Chinese restaurant is a front. Our operatives need to be able to get burner phones at odd hours. The restaurant enables us to get what we need when we need it with no questions asked."

"What kind of life do you live?" she asked, incredulous. "What else is on the menu?"

"Anything. Guns, ammo, cash."

Her eyes bugged. "Cash?"

"Not a lot of cash, just enough to get you around. And it has to be accounted for."

"You mean you have to provide receipts?"

"Sort of."

"Huh. Crazy."

He acknowledged her observation with a brief grunt of agreement. He'd been doing this for so long he'd lost his amazement at how far removed daily operations were from civilian life. He didn't tell her that he also received his assignments from that small Chinese restaurant storefront. The last job had left him questioning too many aspects of his life, which was a liability in his field. He'd actually talked to Tom about it and his friend and mentor had given him solid advice. "The minute you start questioning your objective, you put yourself and the department at risk."

Truer words. How many times had he parroted the same advice to rookies who found they couldn't cut it out there in the field? It was one thing to want the supposed glory of being a sniper, quite another to actually have the stones to pull the trigger without second-guessing your actions.

Jaci accepted the phone and quickly dialed her friend's number. He listened as she carefully gave him instructions on where to meet them but danced around the reason, saying, "You know how you're always looking for the next big challenge? Well, I think I've got one for you. Bring your laptop and all your toys. You're going to need them for this job."

She hung up and handed the phone back. "He's in, and his spidey senses are going nuts. He loves this kind of stuff. He's a genius, and I don't mean that figuratively—he's been a member of Mensa since he was twelve. Computer tech stuff keeps his mental acuity sharp, he says."

"Whatever. We'll see how good he is when he delivers."

"You're such a grouch. He's a good guy. Don't be mean to him. He was there for me when you weren't," she said pointedly, which only served to make him want to punch the guy's lights out. "So behave yourself," she warned him.

Nathan refrained from commenting further and instead pointed to the taco truck. "Lunch," he said and Jaci actually emitted a squeak of happiness as she hurried toward the small truck without shame. At least he knew food could still make her smile.

He allowed himself the small victory—it might be all he could get.

Chapter 8

Jaci and Nathan arrived at the library and found that James was already waiting for them in the room. The minute Jaci walked through the door, James jumped up and folded her in a tight hug, completely ignoring Nathan for the moment. "Geez, girl, you know how to scare a guy. What's going on? Not that I'm not totally intrigued by the opportunity to dig around in other people's playgrounds but something tells me this is big."

Jaci offered a tremulous smile and looked to Nathan. "James, this is Nathan. I don't even know how to explain because I don't understand myself but all I know is that some really dangerous people are after Nathan and me and it's not right for me to ask for your help but I didn't know who else to turn to."

James eyed Nathan with open disapproval, saying to Jaci, "The same Nathan who dumped you, broke your heart and left you homeless?"

Nathan's face colored and his jaw tightened but he allowed Jaci to take the lead. "Yeah, the very same. But we have bigger problems than my love life. Sonia is dead. She was killed right in front of me two nights ago and whoever sent someone to kill me is still out there and we need to figure out why."

"Why would anyone want to kill you? You're a graphic designer, for crying out loud. It's not like you build bombs for a living." He looked to Nathan with open suspicion. "Something tells me this has everything to do with you. Why does somebody want you dead?"

"Your instincts are good." Nathan's mouth twisted in a cold smile. "But they're not good enough to warn you that certain questions shouldn't be asked. Can you do what we ask you to do or not?"

James glowered, clearly not liking Nathan one bit. "Listen, bud, if you're asking me to put my ass on the line you better tell me what I'm up against. I'm willing to help Jaci but I couldn't care less about you. Do you have any idea what she went through when you left her? And now you come around tearing up her life again and you expect me to play nice? Ain't gonna happen."

"James, please," Jaci pleaded with her friend. "I really need your help. I'm not asking you and Nathan to be friends but you are *my* friend and I need your help so please, can you do this for us?"

James and Nathan squared off like two dogs waiting for one another to strike but to her relief James backed off with a dark look sent Nathan's way. "I'm doing this for you, not him." She nodded. He unzipped his laptop and set it up. Within minutes he had a mobile network up and running. "What's this place I'm hacking into?" he asked.

"Burns Mortuary, downtown. Do you know the one?"

James nodded. "My grandfather's service was held there. Nice place. But not exactly big on security, if you know what I mean. Tapping into their system will be like taking candy from a baby."

"We're looking for who took financial responsibility for Olaf Girgich. We need a name and a number." Nathan leaned forward, watching James do his work. "And you need to do it in a way that no one can trace you."

James graced Nathan with a sardonic look. "They don't call me Ghost for nothing. Stand back and watch a master do his work."

Sadly, it didn't take long for James to hack into the mortuary's mainframe. "It scares me how easily you gain access to private material," Jaci admitted softly sharing a look with Nathan. "You make me want to bury my money in a jar in the backyard."

James chuckled. "Not a bad idea. But I don't hack into the banks. Too big of a target." He scanned the information scrolling on the screen, then leaned back with a satisfied smile. "Got it. Your dead guy was cremated with no services and the cremation was paid for by credit card. Don't people realize that a credit card is the easiest way to track someone's whole life? If you have to pay for something, pay with cash."

"Who paid for his services?" Jaci asked.

"Hayes Logistics Inc."

Nathan looked stunned. "Are you sure?" he asked.

"Who is Hayes Logistics?"

"That's a business cover for our department, named after Walter Hayes, our very first director in the U.S. Department of Informational Development, or ID, for short."

"I've never heard of that branch of the government," James said with suspicion. "It sounds made-up."

"And you never will. Part of what makes our department exceptional is the plausible deniability. We get in, we get the job done and we are out. We leave no trace behind."

"Sounds like a good way to get killed and have no one be the wiser," Jaci grumbled and James agreed. She looked at Nathan. "So what now? You already knew that someone in your organization was trying to kill you and me. What does this mean? That they used the company credit card?"

"There are only a few people authorized to use the card and they're all top-level officials."

"Great. So you're saying that not only are we being hunted but we're being hunted by people who are considered untouchable?" Jaci felt ready to throw up. "And here I thought things couldn't get any worse."

"In my experience, things can always get worse. But yeah, that's about the right of it." The crease in Nathan's forehead gave away his concern, which only made Jaci feel worse. Nathan looked to James. "Just how good are your skills?" he asked, challenging him.

James looked affronted. "Better than most. Why?"

"Because if you're as good as you say you are, I have another job for you. It doesn't come without risk. ID has far more security than Burns Mortuary does."

"Are you asking me to break into a government mainframe, possibly putting my life at risk and breaking several known laws that if caught, could land me in federal prison for the rest of my life?"

Jaci shook her head. "No—"

But Nathan overrode her, answering with a firm "Yes."

James held Nathan's stare for a long moment, but Jaci could tell James was tempted. He could never walk away from a challenge like that; at his heart he was a devious little hacker who couldn't pass up the opportunity to put his skills to the test. "Don't do this, James. You've helped us enough. We'll find another way." She looked to Nathan for backup. "You know how dangerous this is. Don't let him take the risk."

"He's a grown man. He can make his own choices. No one is twisting his arm to help us. Are you in?" Nathan was being ruthless.

"I'm in but I can't do it here. I can't get a secure enough line in a public library. Give me a day or two to set it up and we'll meet again at a designated time and place."

"James, this isn't a game. The people after us are killers. I don't want to watch another one of my friends die." Jaci was near tears. "I never should've called you. I'm so sorry."

James's mouth tilted in one of his signature grins that never failed to melt the geeky ladies who fluttered around him. "You always were a worrier," he teased. "No need to stress. No one can catch me. I'm a ghost, remember?"

If Jaci hadn't been ready to lose her lunch right there on the tiled floor of the library she might've laughed at James's chutzpah but as it was she was too stressed to find the humor. She glared at Nathan. "If anything happens to my friend, I swear I will never forgive you."

"I never really thought your forgiveness was ever on the table."

Jaci stared, unable to believe how that one single statement could cause tears to spring to her eyes. She hated to think she could be so easily manipulated but the truth was, her heart leapt at the open regret in Nathan's voice. A needy piece of herself craved the knowledge that Nathan wasn't as stonyhearted as he'd appeared the day he'd tossed her aside and that side was clearly winning over the other side that couldn't care less if Nathan was hurting over what he'd done. Was it even possible that Nathan felt sorry for the pain he'd caused her? She couldn't go down that road—not right now. All that mattered was that no more of her friends died. Well, she didn't want to die, either. No more dying. For anyone. "How will James contact us?" she asked, trying to stay on topic. "You destroyed my phone, remember?"

"Call this number." Nathan scribbled the burner number on a scrap of paper and put it in James's hand. "Only call when you're ready."

James accepted the scrap of paper and tucked it into his pocket. "Yeah, like I'd call you to chat."

Nathan ignored that and directed Jaci out of the room. They left, not so quickly that they would attract notice but to Jaci it felt as if they were running like guilty fugitives.

They were in the truck and heading back up the mountain as quickly as possible. The two-and-a-half-hour drive back to the cabin along a terribly maintained road kept Jaci's thoughts from straying too far into painful territory. But as they walked into the cabin, each silent and engrossed in their own thoughts, Jaci couldn't help but wonder what was going through his head. She'd have given anything at that moment to know if what she'd seen was real or if she'd simply been imagining that somewhere deep down Nathan still cared.

"Did you ever love me?"

Nathan stopped, her question shocking him. He stared a long moment, burning a hole in her soul. She trembled and held that intense gaze without backing down. "Did you ever love me?" she repeated. "I need to know."

The moment stretched painfully long between them and Jaci thought she might suffer from a heart attack before he answered.

"Don't do this," Nathan warned quietly. "It's not going to do either one of us any good to answer that question."

"Why?"

"It just won't. Whether I loved you or not doesn't change the facts. And that's all that matters."

"It matters to me."

Nathan shook his head. "Let it go, Jaci."

Nathan couldn't get out the room fast enough. *Did you ever love me?* With every fiber in his being, with every breath in his body. Didn't she realize that's why he would do anything to protect her? If it were in his power he'd take her so far away from anything that might ever harm her that she'd practically have to live on another planet. That was the irrational side of him, the part that reacted without thought but with pure emotion. In a perfect world he wanted the privilege of sleeping beside her every night, and tickling her until she squealed, and taking her to dinner to watch her order something on the menu only to decide she didn't like it and then pick at his food instead. And when he said it was a privilege, he wasn't exaggerating. Anyone who had the opportunity to be with Jaci should consider it an honor to spend time with her. But it wasn't as if he could admit that as though he was some lovesick teenager. If he were to come out and confess to all of those things then she would ask why he left or why he broke her heart in such a terrible way. And then he'd have to share every little detail of what he'd done in his job, every dirty secret he'd ever kept for ID. And he didn't think he could do that. He didn't want to see the light die in her eyes when she truly processed that he was a killer. Frankly, it was her influence that had made him realize his job wasn't something to be proud of.

Being with Jaci had been like having a light shining on all the dark and musty places in his soul, chasing away the shadows that had lived quite comfortably in all the nooks and crannies.

Nathan wiped at the trickle of sweat beading on his forehead. Central heat and air hadn't been on his list of priorities when he'd purchased the cabin but he couldn't bear to field more of Jaci's questions.

He stripped his shirt and tossed it to the floor. Adrenaline coursed through his veins, making him feel like a junkie, all edgy and filled with nervous energy. His military training kicked in and he dropped to the floor. Without hesitation he pounded out fifty push-ups and then when he felt he couldn't do another rep, he pounded out twenty-five more. Sweat poured down his face and he welcomed the pain in his screaming muscles. Pent-up longing and sexual frustration converged and pushed him to spend the excess energy on physical activity. It wasn't until he'd finished the insane number of push-ups that he realized Jaci was standing in the doorway watching him.

"What are you doing?" he asked, slightly out of breath. He picked up his T-shirt and mopped his face with it. But as he rose to his feet he saw the look in her eyes and his breath quickened. He knew that look. Good God, he knew that look.

How many times had he fantasized about seeing that particular look on Jaci's face again? Too many to count. Too many times he'd woken up in a hot and bothered sweat, his erection springing from his groin as if searching for the woman who was no longer in his bed. "You don't want this," he warned as she advanced. "What you're trying to find is closure. It's not going to happen if we have sex."

Her fingers went to the buttons on her blouse and his breath froze in his chest. "Don't tell me what I need," she murmured, her eyes flashing dangerously. "I need you to shut up and stop being so damn bossy." Her eyes drifted to his jeans. "Now take your pants off."

He swallowed, his hands trembling. He didn't know if he had the strength to refuse her when he wanted her so bad. He was nearly mindless with desire. He took a step back. It was his one shot at doing the right thing and, God help her, she was not making it easy for him. She dropped her blouse to the floor and shimmied out of her jeans. He swallowed a groan. "You're going to regret this," he growled, trying to scare her. "This isn't going to change anything."

He stiffened as she stepped into his space, her hands curling up into his hair. His fingers automatically locked around her waist. "You talk too much," she said, before lifting on her toes and sealing her mouth to his.

Ah, hell... So much for noble intentions.

Chapter 9

Jaci's veins burned with need, which coursed through her body and chased away all trace of reason and plain good sense. She didn't want to think or analyze her actions; she wanted to lose herself in the arms of a man who knew her sexual needs far better than she knew her own. She craved the oblivion that could only be found within the embrace of the one man she had no business being with. But then, as of late, being bad seemed to be her thing, so why not add one more mistake to her list?

She hopped into his arms and he immediately tightened his arms around her behind, hoisting her higher so that the center of her damp heat ground against the rigid muscle of his abdomen. She groaned against his mouth as he gripped her hard, the scent of his male musk surrounding her in a sensual cocoon that ratcheted her desire to another level. "Nathan," she gasped, allowing her head to drop back to allow him better access to her neck. His lips traveled along her skin, nipping and sucking until her body was racked with shudders of wild abandon.

She bit her bottom lip as he carried her to the bed and they tumbled to the soft mattress. The cloying heat inside the bedroom immediately slicked their skin with sweat, which somehow made everything seem that much dirtier and sinfully wonderful at the same time. He dragged her to his mouth and somehow her panties and bra joined his jeans and underwear on the floor. Suddenly they were skin against skin, hands touching and exploring as eagerly as their tongues. He pushed her roughly to her back and she thrilled at his savage touch. She felt helpless beneath his strong, firm hands yet she'd never felt safer. Jaci squeezed her eyes shut as he opened her legs and bared her most feminine place to his gaze.

"Look at me, Jaci," he demanded, his voice a sensual growl that stole her breath as readily as his touch. "I want you to watch as I touch you and know that it's me."

She held her breath and jerked a short nod, loving this dominant little game between them. He'd always been possessive in the bedroom and it delighted her that he remained so with her now, as if no time at all had passed.

His gaze burned a trail straight to her quivering core and she trembled with the force of her need. How had she ever thought anyone else could possibly make love to her the way Nathan did? How many times had she hoped and prayed that someone else would come along to erase the memory of his touch so that she could finally sleep at night without tossing and turning in sexual frustration? Shamefully—too many.

"Your skin is so soft, so sweet," he murmured against her flesh, running his tongue along the damp seam of her feminine folds. She quivered at the intimate contact and gasped as his tongue delved deeper, seeking and finding that hot, swollen pleasure nub with unerring accuracy. As his tongue danced and plunged, his finger penetrated her core, pushing her to her limits until her inner thighs began to tremble and shake as her entire body barreled toward an explosive crash. "That's it, baby…" he said, his tone harsh with lust and desire. "I want to feel you shatter beneath my tongue."

Jaci clutched at the soft pillow, crying out with pleasure as he teased in just the right way until she couldn't stand another moment. Her muscles spasmed and she sucked in a tight breath as every sensation converged on that tightly concentrated area of her body and then radiated outward in a starburst of wonder. "Ohhhh…" She arched and fell back to the bed as Nathan released her, watching her with an approving smile that made her blush.

She slowly came to her senses but before she could completely recover, Nathan rolled her to her side so that she was twisted with her backside exposed and waiting. His large, strong hands caressed her behind with such open appreciation that there was no hiding that he liked what he saw.

Suddenly Nathan paused to roll her to her stomach and she gasped when he jerked her hips up so that she was on her knees. She glanced at him over her shoulder and fresh arousal spiked her blood. With Nathan she'd never felt ashamed or fearful no matter the things they'd done together, and being with him again felt as natural as breathing.

"Oh, Jaci..." he whispered as his tempo became erratic. Her body absorbed the shock of each thrust as her own pleasure began to build. She gripped the quilt, the threading abrading her cheek as the sound of their heavy breathing filled the room. This was heaven, she thought, nearing delirium. She'd accept death at that very moment if it meant she could experience one last second like this. And then as Nathan lost control, Jaci followed a heartbeat later, both shuddering and shaking as they collapsed to the bed, their hearts hammering and their breathing harsh. Had they really just...? Yes. And she still had the slowly receding muscular contractions to prove it.

Their breathing returned to normal just about the same time as Jaci's sanity.

Oh, good gravy...she'd done lost her mind—and her dignity—willfully.

Nathan was stunned. Sex with Jaci had always been exciting but this had been off the charts. He was momentarily speechless. He didn't want to move—he wasn't sure he could even if he'd wanted to. He wanted to sleep. But the heat in the room was nearly suffocating now that he'd expended all that pent-up energy. He rolled to his feet and padded to the window, jerking open the blinds to let in the fresh air and hoping for a small breeze. He glanced at Jaci. "Are you okay?" he asked, as she stared at the ceiling, her glorious red hair fanning out around her on the pillow, her rosy-tipped nipples pebbled beautifully on her upturned breasts. He frowned when she didn't answer and refused to look at him. Instant regret knifed through him as he worried how she was feeling about what they'd done. He'd tried to warn her but she hadn't been willing to listen. "Jaci…I'm s—"

"When you left me I thought the best way to get over you was to date plenty of other guys." She cut into his apology, surprising him with her clear, almost reflective tone. She shifted her gaze to him as she sat up, mindless of her nudity. He scowled, not all that interested in hearing how many other men she'd been with since he'd been gone but before he could say anything, she continued, swinging her legs over the side of the bed and climbing to her feet. "But I've just realized that method never would've worked. There's just something about us that clicks in a way that defies explanation and you can try to deny it but I felt it in my body and I know you felt it, too."

"What's your point?" he asked, hating that he couldn't run from the truth. He agreed with her, but knowing that they were probably soul mates only made the pain worse.

Her eyes narrowed at his curt retort and he bit his tongue before his sex-addled brain made his mouth blurt out how jaw-droppingly gorgeous she looked with her hair tumbled wild from a serious case of sexy bed head and her cheeks ruddy and flushed. *Yeah, stow that.* "I told you nothing would change if we had sex." He tried to focus but Jaci walking around naked was his kryptonite. He made a quick turn and strode to the adjoining bathroom to start the shower, hoping she would take his sudden departure as a sign that he didn't want to continue the conversation. But she simply followed him. "What are you doing?" he asked, bordering on exasperation.

"I'm showering with you."

"I don't think that's a good idea," he said, flipping the water on and averting his stare from roaming her near-perfect curves. How had one woman managed to turn his world upside down?

"Oh, it's a terrible idea," she agreed, the corners of her mouth lifting in a puzzlingly faint smile. "But tell me something I've done in the last two months that remotely resembled a good idea," she challenged. "Tell me something that I don't know."

"C'mon, Jase," he said when she stepped into the shower with a determined expression. Damn her, she knew his weakness when it came to her naked body. Almost unbidden, his hands cupped her full breasts as she went under the spray and his manhood awoke, plumping and strengthening with every heartbeat as blood coursed through his arteries until his erection sprang ready and hard to go again. "Damn you, Jaci. You knew this would happen," he muttered as he descended on her pert nipple, sucking in the tip and pulling her to him. "This is a bad, bad idea," he said with fatalist certainty. But her moan filled his soul with light even if his brain was screaming that loving each other could end up being their death sentence.

"I don't care," she admitted, clinging to him as if she might fall off the earth if she let go. "I might care later but right now, I don't. All I know is being with you is the only thing that feels remotely right in a world that has gone completely bananas. So, yeah, I don't care..." She gazed up at him, her eyes suddenly filling with tears. "Make the world go away, Nathan. Just for a little while."

Her soft plea struck at his heart and he responded with a savage yet tender kiss as he poured all the feelings he couldn't express into that kiss under the spray. He pushed her against the wall, their tongues sliding against one another as he fought a private battle between his heart and mind. Was he wrong for succumbing to the sweetest torture he'd ever known? Probably. And he'd likely end up paying for his pleasure in some horrid way but as he sank into her willing body yet another time, he knew with a certainty that he would've shot anyone who dared come between them in that moment. In that moment, the world belonged to them.

Chapter 10

Jaci pulled her shirt down and maneuvered her still-wet hair over her shoulder to finger-comb the knots as best she could before joining Nathan downstairs. After the shower Nathan had split and she hadn't chased him. Sex was fabulous in the moment but under less than ideal circumstances, the afterglow of happy warm fuzzies faded fairly quickly. She sighed knowing she ought to feel guilty but she didn't. Mostly she felt sad knowing that as great as they were between the sheets, loving each other wasn't an option. As she descended the stairs, she resolved to shelve anything that didn't help them stay alive because now was not the time to sort out their lingering issues.

"Find anything?" she asked when she saw him at

his laptop, his expression dark. "Why does my stomach hurt just thinking of what could possibly put that look on your face?"

Nathan leaned back, frustrated. "I'm hitting a brick wall. I don't know where to start. I've been racking my brain trying to think why someone within my own organization might want me dead, and I'm stumped."

"Really?"

"Why do you find that shocking?" he asked with a faint scowl.

She shrugged, going for honesty. "You're not exactly a people person, Nathan. Sometimes you're surly, prickly and anti-social. Actually, now that I think about it, I'm surprised there aren't a multitude of people who'd want to put you down like a rabid dog."

"Thanks." He returned his attention back to his laptop and Jaci took a seat beside him. He cast her a short look, saying, "I doubt there's much you can do to help. Why don't you read a magazine or something?"

"And now you can add me to that list of people who wouldn't mind seeing you take a bullet," she quipped with irritation. "Listen, you need a fresh perspective. In my design work, when I can't get a design right, I take a step back and get someone else's opinion, mainly James's because we live together." Nathan's jaw hardened and Jaci was secretly thrilled that Nathan was just a bit jealous. Served him right for letting her go. She continued as if she hadn't noticed his reaction. "And usually with the input from fresh eyes, I can figure it out. That's what you need. Fresh perspective."

"And how do you suppose I get that? It's not as if I can sit down and chat with a coworker about something like this."

"I know I'm not ideal in your mind, but I can try and help. I'm not completely useless, you know."

"I know you're not useless, Jase," he said. "But—"

"But nothing. I can take it. You think I'm this fragile woman who will fall apart if I hear something scary about your work and in all fairness, before all this terrible stuff had happened to me, I might've. But my world has been torn apart and if I want to have any hope of putting it back together again, I need to stay strong. Which means you have to stop babying me."

He regarded her for a long moment and she pressed a little harder. "I can take it, Nathan. I promise. Please let me help in some way. I can't sit here and do nothing. It will drive me insane and I will take you with me."

At that he chuckled wryly and she offered a tentative smile. "Okay. I guess you're right," he said with a sigh. "Where do you want to start?"

"At the beginning," she answered, shocking him. "I want to know how you got your start in this business, all the way to the point where we're running for our lives."

"You sure about that?"

"Nathan, we're broken up. It doesn't matter what you tell me at this point. The idea is to stay alive, right?" He nodded and she settled in with a deep breath, determined to remain true to her declaration. "Okay, I'm ready."

She hoped.

* * *

She was ready, but was he? Nathan wasn't sure how sharing his dirty secrets would help but since he was flummoxed and frustrated by his lack of progress, he was almost desperate.

"How about the *Reader's Digest* version instead of the *War and Peace* epic saga?" he asked, not relishing the idea of sharing his past. If he could get it over with quickly with the abridged version, that was fine by him. She accepted his request and he started. "My family sucked. Typical family drama—Dad was a mean drunk and Mom was a sloppy drunk. I have a younger brother somewhere but we lost contact when I split the roost. Last I heard he was living in Florida, or something like that."

"You have a brother? Why haven't you tried to stay in touch?"

"Seemed easier to simply cut ties," he admitted, remembering his brother's panicked expression when he'd walked out the door after the latest fight with the old man. He'd been seventeen and Jake had been fifteen. He hated the guilt that dogged him but he'd always told himself that Jake was better off striking out on his own with nothing holding him back, including pissed-off older brothers with something to prove to the world. "Besides, I was hell-bent on joining the Marines. I didn't want to worry about who I was leaving behind."

"Don't you think that's kinda harsh?" she asked.

He cast her a dark look. "How about no passing

judgment during Story Hour, okay?" he said and she immediately pretended to zip her lip. "The thing is, I've always felt guilty about Jake but in my line of work, having ties is a liability. And I didn't want to do that to Jakey."

"Noble," she said, forgetting her promise to keep her mouth shut. God love her, he should've known that would be impossible for someone like Jaci. "So… Any other siblings you cut from your life in order to *protect* them?"

"No," he answered with a glower. She made him sound like an even bigger ass than he'd been. "I had a sister but she died when she was six."

Jaci gasped and her stricken expression made him wish he hadn't shared. "How awful. What happened?" she asked.

"It's not important," he said, waving off her concern. He definitely didn't want to talk about Bunny but one look at Jaci's face and he knew she wouldn't let it go. He could've shut her down forcefully but he supposed there was no need to hide his past now. "My sister Krista—we called her Bunny—died when my drunken mother backed over her with the station wagon we used to own. I was supposed to be watching her but me and Jake were arguing over something stupid and I didn't see her go outside. All I remember after that is the screaming."

"How awful for your family." She placed a hand gently on his shoulder, but her compassionate gaze made him shift with discomfort and he shrugged her touch away. He didn't deserve her compassion. She withdrew her hand as if he'd bitten her. He immediately felt like a jerk but she didn't give him a chance to apologize. "So you left home at seventeen and I assume you joined the military?"

"I wasn't old enough to join so I did odd jobs to stay alive and slept on friends' couches until the day I turned eighteen. I enlisted and never looked back."

She clearly struggled with questions she wanted to ask but she held them back, sticking to the relevant parts, for which he was inordinately grateful. He hadn't talked about Bunny in over twenty years and he was surprised by how much it still hurt to talk about her. Bunny had been such a cool kid; funny and cute but she'd also been a bit of a handful, particularly for a ten-year-old who was trying to be father and mother to two younger siblings without any clue as to what the hell he was doing.

"How did you become a sniper?" Jaci asked.

"I'd served a few tours in Iraq and Afghanistan and I'd gained a reputation for being a crack shot. A commander for the Marine Scout Sniper School called me one day when I was stateside again and said he'd heard good things about me. I graduated at the top of my class and then just as I was heading to a briefing for my first assignment, Tom Wyatt, the director of ID, approached me with a job offer. The commander and Wyatt went way back and he'd put in a good word for me. The money was better than I'd ever dreamed of as a basic enlisted man, and I didn't have anyone else to worry about but myself. I started with ID a few weeks later."

"Did you know you were going to be killing people as part of your job description?"

"I didn't," he admitted, almost afraid to answer truthfully but she'd said she could handle it if he did. "But when I was given my first kill order, I didn't hesitate. In fact, I was determined to succeed. I wanted to prove to Tom Wyatt that he'd made the right choice in taking a chance on me. I owe a lot to Tom. He took me under his wing, for whatever reasons I don't know, but he taught me a lot about honor and integrity."

"So, in a way, Tom was like a father figure to you?" He hadn't thought of it that way but now that Jaci had pointed it out, he supposed she was right and he nodded in agreement. "Have you talked to Tom about what's happening? Maybe he can help."

"No," he answered, shaking his head. "I don't want to get Tom involved until I absolutely have to."

"But he might be in danger, too. Especially if this person is a high enough ranking official within the organization to use the department credit card. You'd feel terrible if you didn't tell him and then he ended up getting hurt," she pointed out.

"I just want more to go on before saying something," he said. "Plus, I don't want to tip off whoever's responsible by going to Tom prematurely."

"Well, I hate to break it to you but we don't have the luxury of carefully building a case. If we wait too long, we might end up dead."

"Hard to argue that logic," he said grimly. He cast Jaci an apprising glance. "Pretty levelheaded for an artistic type in an extreme situation," he said by way of a compliment. "I expected you to faint or something."

"Thanks. I think." She drew a deep breath. "Well, sometimes I surprise myself. I hate that saying 'what doesn't kill you, makes you stronger,' because a lot of well-meaning people tried to tell me that when we broke up and I was a total mess. I didn't get dressed for weeks." She paused as if realizing she didn't want to share her lowest moment with him. But instead of stopping, she met his gaze and lifted her chin, saying, "James really helped me get through the worst of it and honestly, the man deserves a medal for braving the stench of my depression."

Nathan felt a scowl coming on but he tried to hold it in check for Jaci's sake. It was bad enough he'd been responsible for her pain; the least he could do was to stomach more praise of the glorious roommate, James.

When she realized he was giving her the space to share, she continued. "But maybe our breakup was a blessing in disguise because I don't know how I'd have handled this latest crisis without having been through the pain of losing you. So, I guess...thank you."

He scowled. "Don't thank me for breaking your heart."

She shrugged and returned to the topic at the core of the conversation but he was caught between the urge to explain his reasoning and letting it go. In the end he swallowed his urge to explain his thought process and followed her lead.

"Okay, so you killed people.... About how many in your career?" she asked.

"God, Jase...how is that relevant?" he asked, extremely uncomfortable with that particular question. "That's not something I brag about."

"Of course not. I'd be worried if you did. My reason for asking is because maybe the key to who's after us is related to an assignment."

Wow, he hoped not. "If that were the case, we'd be screwed. I have no way of researching that information beyond what was given to me for the initial case."

"Maybe not. We might only have to backtrack a few years. I mean, presumably whoever is interested in killing you hasn't been stewing for the past ten years, right? I don't know for sure but if someone were interested in hurting you, wouldn't they want to do it relatively quickly?"

"Not necessarily. Maybe they were waiting for the right moment," he said.

She frowned. "Seems kind of weird to wait years to exact revenge on someone but I'm an impatient person so maybe my perspective is skewed. If I was mad enough to kill someone, I'd want to get it over with before I lost my nerve."

Nathan swallowed a small chuckle at the idea of Jaci trying to kill someone. She was so tenderhearted she grimaced when she swatted flies. However, something about her logic sparked his memory. He leaned forward and logged on to his computer again, accessing the file for a job he did right before he and Jaci broke up.

Jaci noted his change in demeanor. "Did you remember something?" she asked, leaning forward to look over his shoulder.

"Maybe," he answered, then realized in order to explain his gut feeling, he'd have to explain the true reason they'd broken up and he didn't want to do that.... Not yet. He closed his laptop and looked to Jaci, saying, "I need to do a little digging on my own and I don't want to put you at risk."

"Nathan, we already covered this," she said with a small sound of impatience. "You can't protect me from every little thing that isn't to my liking. I'm not made from porcelain and I resent you treating me as if I'm a fragile basket case. Frankly, I'm beginning to wonder how you saw me if you think I was this unstable."

"I don't think you're unstable but I hid a lot from you, Jase."

"If you don't think that I've already figured that out, you're insane. You have no reason to hide anything from me anymore. Just spit it out, already. I promise I won't go into hysterics."

"I will but I need to do it on my own timetable, and not be pressured into it," he said.

"Sorry, but in case you haven't noticed, we don't have the luxury of time. Just treat me as you would a coworker," she suggested and he stared, wondering if she'd lost her marbles. Jaci? A coworker? Even if he hadn't just spent a good couple of hours doing the mattress mambo with her, there was no way he'd ever consider Jaci as anything resembling a peer. Not because she wasn't smart or capable but because he didn't want to contaminate what he held in his heart for her. Ugh. Next he'd be spouting poetry and throwing rose petals at her feet. "I need more time, okay?" he said a bit brusquely as he rose and she followed with a frown marring her beautiful face. "What?" he asked.

"You're doing it again. Damn it, Nathan, when are you going to trust me?" she asked, plainly disappointed with his decision to shut her down. "This isn't fair. I can't just sit back and pretend that we're vacationing in the middle of nowhere while you play the hero."

She searched his gaze for a long moment, waiting for him to capitulate, but he wouldn't—not on this. When he told her the truth about everything that had led up to their breakup, it would ruin any sense of stability she had left. It was bad enough that she'd seen her best friend die right in front of her and he'd had to drag her from her life. Time would come soon enough that she'd have to know the truth but maybe, if he were lucky, he'd find the son of a bitch behind all this and end everything before he'd have to share the details.

"You might be ready, but I'm not," he told her, and left it at that. He knew she didn't like his answer but that was too bad. "Are you hungry?" he asked and was rewarded with a dark look for his trouble.

Before he could say anything else, Jaci gave up in

disgust and walked away. Nathan let her go with an inward sigh.

Ah, hell, why couldn't she just leave it be?

Chapter 11

Jaci had planned to spend some time cooling off but she'd realized if she didn't say anything, he'd never answer questions. Nathan was a fan of "ignore it and it will go away," but she wasn't. Determined to shake some answers out of the man, she went back downstairs.

Nathan looked up from his computer as she descended the steps, surprised. "Did you change your mind about eating? I thought we could make something together." She knew this was his attempt at a peace offering but food was the last thing on her mind.

"When we broke up you said that you were bored and you just couldn't be with me any longer. But then you started watching my every move like some deranged stalker, which is how you knew I was in trouble that night in the alley." She hesitated before continuing. "And there's one more thing.... The way you touched me—makes me wonder a few things."

"Such as?" he asked, his gaze narrowing with dislike at her rendition of events thus far. She ignored his scowl and continued.

"I think you lied about your feelings. Why did you break up with me?"

Nathan sighed. "Jaci, I already told you I don't want to talk about that. Don't you think we have bigger problems?"

She nodded. "Absolutely. But you won't let me help and you won't answer questions about the case, so that leaves me with dealing with the questions that have always been in my mind. And since we have nothing to do, no television to watch, no phones...I might as well get the answers to questions that are of a personal nature."

Nathan looked as if he'd rather eat nails but she didn't feel sorry for him one bit. He'd brought this on himself. If he would just open up to her and tell her the freaking truth maybe they could get past all of this. She settled on the sofa with an expectant expression. "I'm ready when you are."

"You want me to admit that I lied? Yes, you're right. The reasons I told you for breaking up were not truthful. But does it really matter? The bottom line is we couldn't be together. As far as I'm concerned that's all that still matters."

"Well, I disagree. I want to know why you broke up with me. Right now."

"I won't tell you."

"I won't stop asking."

They squared off, a test of wills with no obvious victor, and she knew Nathan hoped she would give up. But she was stronger than she was before and she'd learned a few things. "You can try to steamroll me but it's not going to work. Your actions don't make sense. One minute you're breaking my heart and the next minute you're saving my life. You're crazy if you think that I can't put two and two together."

He scowled, his voice rising. "You are the most difficult, irritating, stubborn woman I've ever met. Haven't you ever heard the saying 'curiosity killed the cat'?"

"I'm not a cat. Quit changing the subject."

A crease appeared between his brows and if she wasn't mistaken, he began to sweat, which she found amusing. The big bad gunman was squirming. And was she a terrible person for enjoying that?

"I'll tell you what I think. You broke up with me because of something that happened with your job. Not because you stopped loving me or because you couldn't stand the idea of monogamy but because you were trying to protect me from something. Am I right?"

"Yes, damn it. Are you satisfied? Is that what you wanted to hear? Yes, I still care for you and I don't want to see you get hurt but it doesn't change the fact that we can't be together. I will walk away from you as soon as I know that this is finished. So don't get any ideas that we're riding off into the sunset together."

Oh, the nerve of that man. "What makes you think I would ride off into the sunset with you? Regardless of the reasons why you broke up with me, the fact remains you broke my heart. I just wanted to know the reasons why. I believe I'm entitled to at least that."

At her pointed statement he had the grace to look chagrined. A moment of charged silence passed between them and then he said, "I was just trying to keep you safe."

"Well, it didn't work, did it?" Jaci looked away. "So let's try something new. No more lies. No more evasion. Just try leveling with me and see how that works."

Nathan held her stare as if assessing her ability to handle whatever he could throw at her and when her gaze didn't waver he relented. "Okay," he capitulated with a sigh. "But if I agree to tell you everything, you have to stop questioning my decisions. My ability to keep you safe is directly related to your ability to listen and obey. Without question."

"I have an issue with that word 'obey,'" she said, narrowing her stare and wondering how the hell she'd manage to blindly follow someone she didn't really trust any longer. But she supposed he had a point. She nodded grudgingly. "Okay. I'll try." He seemed to understand that was the best that she could offer and accepted with an abbreviated nod. One battle won, now for the war. She drew a deep breath and prepared herself. "I want to know about the real Nathan Isaacs, not the carefully crafted cover version of the man. I'm ready."

The prospect of telling Jaci everything made Nathan's stomach cramp. He hadn't been held accountable to another human being in his personal life since he'd walked out the front door of his parents' home. He told himself he preferred the role of the lone wolf, answering to no one. But as Jaci sat there waiting for him to begin he couldn't escape the feeling that he was about to change the game by confessing his sins.

"When we met I was on sabbatical," he began, rising because he couldn't bear to sit still while he shared details of the past. "Tom had said that I needed a break. I'd done a blitz of assignments and he worried that I was heading for burnout. Considering I was his top sniper, he said he wanted to protect the department's assets. At first I didn't want the rest. Somehow the suggestion to take a break had seemed like I'd done something wrong but Tom made me realize that everyone needed a little R & R now and then, so I agreed to a one-month break. And that's when I met you."

"At the coffee shop," she said in a soft tone as she shared the memory from her perspective. "Sometimes for a change of scenery I liked to go to the coffee shop to work. I like to people watch. And you fascinated me the minute you walked through the door."

"With that red hair, you were hard to miss." Nathan refrained from telling her that the minute he'd seen her, everyone else in the coffee shop had disappeared. She'd been wearing a snow-white sweater that had made her red hair all the more brilliant, and jeans that hugged her curves and made him want to get a handful of that amazing body. In short, she'd set his blood on fire. He cleared his throat to remind himself to stick to only the necessary parts of the story and continued. "And we started talking."

"You asked me what I was drinking—"

"Chai tea latte, extra whipped cream and no foam," he remembered with ease. Jaci, he would learn, had a raging sweet tooth. She bit her lip in an endearing manner at his sharp memory and he had to force himself to keep in mind what was at stake. "One thing led to another and we went on a date or two, which lead to so many more I lost count. My whole sabbatical was taken with trying to find more ways to spend time with you," he admitted.

"Yeah, same here. I put off a lot of clients that month." She laughed. "I'd never met anyone like you."

He could believe that but she'd had no idea just how true that statement was. He cleared his throat and focused. It was easy to recall the good stuff—there'd been plenty of memories to choose from—but Jaci knew about those. He had to shed light on the dark places. "You remember that night someone broke into your place?" he asked, getting straight to the point.

She frowned. "Yeah. You surprised a burglar in my apartment," she said, then paled. "Are you telling me that was no burglar?"

He nodded reluctantly.

"Then, who was it?" she whispered, almost afraid to ask.

"I never found out who he was—he managed to hit me with a surprise left and bail out the window, but he dropped the knife on his way out."

"How do you know he wasn't a thief, though? They can carry weapons."

"Generally speaking, burglars take the easy stuff. Jewelry, electronics and other easily grabbed items. Nothing was touched and there was cash lying on the dresser in the bedroom. No," he said certainly, "that man was there to kill you or me. Possibly both. It was sheer luck that I got there before you."

She shuddered, unable to hide her reaction to her first brush with near death. "Do you think it was the same guy in the alley?" she asked.

"No. This guy was smaller and more agile. The guy in the alley was a thug."

"Why didn't you tell the police that you thought he was more than a burglar?"

"Because if I had told the police my suspicions, they would've wanted to know why and there's no easy way to explain what I do for a living. Not to mention one of our directives is to always fly under the radar, which would've been impossible if I hadn't lied. Besides, I had a better chance of finding the guy than the police ever would."

Her brows rose in question. "Did you?"

He scowled. “No. And I searched high and low for the bastard. Someone was protecting him.”

“Which goes back to our original question—who is trying to kill you? If all of this started back in June, wouldn’t it be a reasonable theory that whatever got this ball rolling has something to do with that time period? What jobs did you do during that time?”

Nathan didn’t need to think hard. The last three assignments he’d done for ID had left a bad taste in his mouth. It wasn’t his job to question, and in the past he’d had no problem following orders, but something tripped his gut instinct and he found himself asking more questions than might have been prudent. “There was a guy named Harry Winslow—something about the job didn’t seem right. I took my concerns to Tom but he assured me that looks were deceiving and that Winslow was bad guy.”

“How so? I mean, what did he do that was so bad that the government had to put him down?” Jaci asked, dubious. “Please don’t tell me it was something like cheating on his taxes. That’s a scary thought.”

“On the surface Winslow was the owner of a start-up pharmaceutical company that manufactured drugs that artificially boosted the immune system for people who were undergoing cancer treatments. It was supposed to be cutting-edge stuff. But while Winslow was accepting accolades for his company’s research, he was also the main funding source for several opium fields in Afghanistan. I don’t know if you know anything about the opium wars in the Middle East but it’s ugly. I've seen atrocities you can't even imagine done in the name of greed."

He paused and ran his finger along his eyebrow as he suffered through an echo of the turmoil he'd experienced as he surveyed his hit. "Military men follow orders, and that's what I did. But I liked to think that each of my targets deserved what was coming to them." He shrugged. "But after Winslow… I don't know, maybe that wasn't the case."

"What do you mean?"

"Winslow kept his nose clean. I watched him for weeks but I never caught him doing anything remotely criminal. Phone records, surveillance, internet traffic, you name it, I had access to everything but nothing tripped my alarm. The man had simply seemed dedicated to his work at the pharmaceutical company." Nathan sighed, shaking his head at the lingering doubt in his mind. "In the end, I did the job and walked away. It was shortly after that Tom suggested I needed a break."

"Have you ever considered…" She lifted her gaze to his, searching. "Maybe Winslow wasn't guilty at all? Maybe he was innocent and you were lied to so that you would do someone else's dirty work?"

He refused to believe it. "No. You have no idea the channels that have to be operating in perfect tandem to get a kill order passed through. It's a complicated checks and balances system so that no one can take advantage."

"Are you saying that there's no way a government entity can be corrupted?" At her sardonic tone he frowned, not liking the questions that rose fresh in his mind. "Listen, I think you need to focus on finding out more about Winslow and what he was working on. Maybe the answer we're looking for is in that case file."

"I don't have access to the internal files. I wonder if your friend Ghost is having any luck breaking into the ID database?"

"If anyone can do it, James can. What do we do in the meantime?"

"I think I need to talk to Tom."

Jaci nodded gravely. "I think you're right."

Nathan rubbed his chin and muttered an expletive. Why did the prospect of talking to Tom again about this case give him a serious bad feeling?

He supposed there was only one way to find out.

"But before we go to Tom, there's someone else I want to talk to. Someone who, I think, has already walked in my shoes."

Chapter 12

Jaci followed Nathan's lead and flattened herself against the brick wall of an older building, closing her eyes against the images of Sonia dying in an alley much like the one they were hiding in right now, while Nathan rapped three times on the warped metal door. "Where are we?" she whispered, swallowing the lump of fear that seemed caught in her windpipe. It was one thing to boldly proclaim you were ready for whatever may come, but quite another to actually face possible death around every corner. Jaci had already squeaked twice when startled, earning an annoyed look from Nathan and she was resolved to be less freaked out by shadows and creepy noises.

"I have a friend who owns the bar," he answered, waiting for someone to come to the door. "This door leads straight to his main office upstairs. He always keeps a guard posted on the other side, just in case someone gets it in their head to try and pry it open to gain access."

"Why would anyone want to break into a seedy bar on the wrong side of town?" she asked, glancing dubiously around at the trash littering the ground. "I think even the homeless have higher standards."

"Nothing is ever as it seems in my world, Jaci," he reminded her and she nodded, feeling quite naive and not at all as worldly as she'd hoped when she'd convinced him that she could handle whatever he tossed her way. The door opened and a big, burly man without a neck to speak of stared them down with fists clenched. "Bar entrance is on Fifth and Martin," he intoned dangerously, gesturing for them to move on before they got a fistful of knuckle meat for their trouble.

Nathan ignored the threat. "Tell Miko that Nathan Isaacs needs to speak with him—it's urgent."

The bouncer eyed him with open suspicion. Miko paid his men well. If Nathan didn't pass the test, they'd be left standing out in the sweltering heat with bootprints on their butts for their trouble. "Password."

"Sierra Alpha Foxtrot Echo," he answered without blinking. The thug moved aside and they slipped inside to bound up the stairs to a small office above the raucous din of the bar below.

Miko, a man in his mid-thirties who'd once been an operative within ID and had since retired, relaxed from behind the desk when he saw Nathan. "Ever thought of picking up a phone, friend? You almost got your nuts shot off." At that he lifted the gun hidden under the desk and returned it to the drawer. Nathan quirked the barest of smiles and closed the door for privacy. "Ah, so it's like that? How did I know someday you'd show up with your ass in hot water?"

"Because you know me well enough—I don't quit or give up, even when the odds are against me," he answered, slapping his friend in a quick, manly bear hug. They broke apart and Nathan surveyed Miko with a grin. "You're getting soft. Too much desk work and too many beers. When was the last time you lifted anything but a pen?"

"Screw you, Nathan. I can bench your scrawny frame any day of the week," Miko boasted with a wink to Jaci as he moved away to focus on her. "And who might you be? Aside from the woman of my dreams?" he asked, stopping only when Nathan made a low growl. "Oh? Taken? Far be it from me to piss on another man's territory."

Jaci gasped and muttered something that sounded a lot like *gross!* and Nathan swallowed the chuckle at her disgust. Trained killers often had a skewed sense of humor…and justice. Nathan knew he could trust Miko with his life. He'd spent many nights in various places of hell with the man at his side. Miko returned to his chair and leaned back, his dark eyes sharp as a needle point even if his pose seemed laid back. "So what's going on? You just here for a visit or what?"

"Take a guess."

"Someone is trying to kill us," Jaci blurted out, tired of the back and forth. "Someone within ID is after us and we need your help to figure out who."

"Is this true?" Miko asked, suddenly serious.

Nathan shot Jaci an irritated look but otherwise nodded in response. "Yeah, that's about the long and short of it. Someone is apparently tired of my company and wants me gone."

"Yeah, they're brutal like that," Miko muttered, glancing away. "How do you know it's someone within ID? Fact is, with your credentials, I'd think it fair to say you've pissed off your share of people."

"True," Nathan allowed but added, "But we have pretty solid evidence that someone high in the food chain signed the kill order."

"What evidence?"

"Someone is using the company credit card to pay for the thugs," Jaci jumped in, eager to add something of value.

Miko looked to Jaci, then to Nathan. "Want to introduce me to your lady friend here?" he asked with the guise of manners, though Nathan knew he wanted to discern her value and trustworthiness before he spoke freely.

"Jaci Williams, meet Miko Archangelo. Miko, meet my ex-girlfriend, and no, she's not interested in exchanging phone numbers," he warned his friend with a meaningful scowl. Miko had always had a weakness for beautiful women and although Nathan would trust him with his life, he wouldn't trust the man further than he could punt him around Jaci.

Miko chuckled and winked at Jaci, saying, "Someone's got this old soldier all tied up in knots. If I didn't know better, I'd say you were still his squeeze."

She blushed and possibly for the first time in her life wisely remained silent, looking to Nathan for direction, which he took, getting to the point. "I need to talk to you about the Constantin job," he said, knowing Miko would rather chew bullets than talk about his last year with ID. As he expected, Miko shut down, his gaze shuttering.

"What's to tell? I was tired of it all. I became a liability in the field and a danger to my team." He forced a smile. "Besides, I like being a bar owner. No one is trying to kill me and I still make money. God bless the drunks out there keeping me clothed and housed."

"You and I both know that you didn't quit because you lost your touch. You were an excellent marksman and you never missed."

Miko smiled but his eyes were hard as he reached into his desk and pulled out two glasses and bottle of Jameson. He poured and pushed a glass to Nathan before he lifted his own glass to his lips and swallowed all of the amber liquid in one gulp. "Read the file. I retired with full honors. I've even got medical and dental for life." He poured another and eyed Nathan. "You didn't come here to pick apart my history. What are you here for, Nathan?" he asked.

Nathan was almost afraid to voice the niggling

fear in the back of his head because if he did, it might make everything that much more real. But they hadn't come so he could chew the fat with an old friend. "I think whoever is after me within ID wants me dead to cover up an assignment that never should've been sanctioned."

"What do you mean?" Miko asked quietly, his fingers stilling as he traced the rim of his glass.

"I think, hell, I don't know for sure, but someone high up is considering me a loose end. The last three assignments from ID left me feeling uneasy but Tom assured me everything was solid. I don't like the questions that are circling my brain."

"Because if you can't trust the people who have your back, the ones who tell you that you're not just killing innocent people but doing a service to your country, then who can you trust, right?" Miko's sardonic twist of his lips spoke volumes and Nathan felt his stomach pitch.

"Your last assignment… What happened?"

"I bugged out. Something didn't feel right and I knew I couldn't back out without a real good reason—and no good enough reason existed as far as Tom was concerned." Miko tossed back another drink as if needing the liquid courage to admit his sins. "I didn't mean to do so much damage but when the car flipped, I lost control and ended up flying through the windshield. Broke my arm in five places." He ran his finger along his forearm showing where the scars remained. "It sucked but I was alive. And the best part? I was out of ID. My trigger finger was out of commission. The surgery was able to put me back together again but I'd lost my stability. I couldn't hold steady any longer. Discharged on a medical with full honors. Happy ending."

Nathan remembered the wreck but had never had any idea Miko had crashed his car purposefully just to get free from ID. "Why didn't you tell me?" he asked.

"No point. Besides, it was time for me to get out. My heart wasn't in the job anymore."

"You suspected the assignment was bogus, didn't you?" Nathan pressed. "That's why you bugged out." At Miko's pursed lips but otherwise silent response, Nathan felt his world reel. "Did you share your concerns with anyone?" he asked. Miko shook his head and Nathan breathed a sigh of relief. He used to think his world was safe because he knew what was out there, but now...nothing felt safe. "You taking precautions?"

"Do you think I keep that thug at my back door just because I like his company? Hell, yes, I've taken precautions. But you and I both know if ID wants me dead, it's gonna happen no matter what I do. Men like you and me are the best at what we do and ID has plenty of guys just waiting to make their mark within the department."

"Why didn't you leave the city?"

"And go where?" He shrugged. "I've always wanted to own a bar and now I do. If my time is up, at least I'm going to go out doing something I enjoy." He sighed and stared at Nathan and Jaci with grim certainty. "Maybe it's time for you and the redheaded beauty here to split town for a while, let things settle down. Maybe whoever wants you dead will figure you're not worth the trouble."

"I'm not leaving until I figure out who's behind this. If someone is using ID to do their dirty work, it needs to stop," Nathan said.

"I used to like playing the hero, too. Careful, buddy. It's addictive and it can end up getting you killed."

Nathan grabbed his shot of whiskey and downed it in one swallow. "I'm not playing the hero. It's personal. Whoever put this plan in motion forgot one thing—I don't stop until the job is done. And I'm not stopping until I have the person responsible for messing with my life in my crosshairs."

"Stubborn ass," Miko muttered. "That quality is going to put you in the ground with your lady friend right beside you."

Jaci surprised them both when she stood and said resolutely, "Nothing is going to happen to us. Nathan is the best and I believe in him. If he says he's going to catch whoever is doing this, he will." She looked to Nathan. "Are we done?"

Nathan nodded and rose, casting a look at Miko. "Stay safe, man."

In answer, Miko lifted his newly filled shot glass in mock salute. "I ain't worried. I'm just a bar owner. You're the one who needs to watch his back."

Wasn't that the truth. But as Nathan and Jaci sprinted for the truck tucked away in the shadows,

Nathan couldn't shake the feeling that that was the last time he'd ever see his friend.

Someone was intent on cleaning up loose ends and that included anyone who'd ever raised a hand in question over jobs that should've been sanctioned by the proper channels but may not have been what they seemed.

That sick feeling in his gut had just intensified.

Chapter 13

The blanket of silence in the truck was enough to smother an elephant. Jaci sent a furtive glance at Nathan and even in the shadows, she could see the hard set of his jaw as he processed the information his friend had shared. Questions swirled in her brain but she was afraid to voice them until Nathan started the conversation first. However, as the moments stretched on with no sound from Nathan, she realized she was going to have to take the plunge.

"Do you trust Miko?" she ventured cautiously, trying to get a feel for the direction of Nathan's thoughts.

"Yeah," he bit out, his eyes never leaving the road as he negotiated a tight turn and then took a side street off the main highway.

"So what does this mean? If Miko left ID because he didn't trust the integrity of the people in charge… does this mean…" She let the rest of her question trail but she knew Nathan was wondering the same thing. "What are you going to do?"

"After talking to Miko, I know I don't have a choice but to talk to Tom."

Jaci appeared worried. "I know. But it seems to me that Tom is the common denominator in all this. He's the one who assured you you were doing the right thing when clearly you had doubts and doubly so for your friend Miko. I hate to break it to you but I think Tom might be the bad guy in this scenario."

"You don't know Tom like I do. He would never betray his team," he said hotly. "He's been like a father to me ever since I joined ID. If something is rotten in the department, he deserves to know."

"And what if Tom is the one who's pulling the strings and going to him just puts your life in more danger? And, by proxy, mine? Why don't we wait and see what James has dredged up before we go half-cocked to your director, who may or may not be involved?" It seemed a reasonable request by her standard but Nathan looked stubbornly set in his way of thinking, which only gave her a serious case of impending diarrhea. "Please, Nathan?" she pleaded and he relented with a short jerk of his head. It wasn't a gracious capitulation on his part but she'd take it. "Thank you," she said, wishing she could reach over and smooth that frown from his face but knowing he wouldn't welcome the contact right now. She could only imagine the turmoil going on in his brain knowing that the man he trusted the most might be the enemy. She didn't envy his pain but she knew how it felt to be betrayed.

"Call your buddy," Nathan instructed tersely. "I'm only going to wait for so long before going to Tom."

"But James said he'd call us if he had information," she protested with a frown. "Shaking his chain isn't going to make him work any faster. This is delicate stuff."

"I don't care. Call him."

Jaci scowled and pulled a different burner phone from her purse and dialed James's number. It went to voice mail and she hung up. "No answer." She bit her lip, worried. "Do you think James is okay? Should we check on him?"

"We'll wait another hour then call him again."

"What are we going to do in the city for an hour while we wait? It's not like we can drive around all night, and the cabin is too far to make a temporary trek," she pointed out.

"I know a place we can go."

"Where?"

"The city is loaded with safe houses owned by ID There's one near here that is usually unoccupied because it's one of the older places that isn't listed on the manifest any longer."

"Why didn't we go there in the first place?" she asked.

"Because there are a handful of people who know

about this place, but no one knows about my cabin in the mountains. Call me paranoid but I liked having that extra layer of separation."

She nodded, her head spinning at the layers she'd only just begun to peel back on what constituted Nathan's life. It made her wonder how he'd ever imagined he could start a life with another person. Maybe he hadn't and every word that had ever crossed his lips had been a lie. "Did you ever plan to stay with me or was I just a temporary diversion from your patriot games?" she asked, unable to stop her mouth.

"Jaci…don't start," he warned with a subtle weariness to his tone that immediately set her off.

"You can't shut me down each time I ask you a question that you don't want to answer. I deserve information, especially when your misinformation wrecked my life."

"Why do you always pick the most inopportune time to dig into the past? You make it nearly impossible for me to protect your feelings."

"I don't want you to protect my feelings. Please, God, don't protect me any longer! Don't you realize that it was your attempt to protect me that hurt me the most?"

Nathan startled her when he slammed his hand against the steering wheel, his voice rising. "Yes! What am I supposed to do? Say I'm sorry? Okay, yes I'm sorry for hurting you. But right now I'm trying to keep you alive! Doesn't that register in your brain? Why don't we just agree that I was an ass and leave it at that. End of story. Done. I'm the bad guy and you're my innocent victim. Satisfied?"

"You self-righteous jerk. And no, you don't get off that easily. If you're going to attempt an apology, you need to start with a real one, not some half-baked spouting off in a fit of anger because you feel defensive. And, honestly, I don't think I'd accept an apology just yet. I want answers. I want to know why you started a relationship with me when you had no intentions of following through. Were you just looking for a one-night stand or a quick fling for your vacation? You could've been honest from the start. Then at least I would have been aware that your heart was never an option."

"I didn't string you along." Nathan rubbed the steering wheel where he'd slapped it. "You were a game changer in my life. That's what I've been trying to tell you. Everything that has happened up until this point has been me trying to protect you *from* my life. I never wanted you to get mixed up in the situations that have happened. I want you to go on living your life as you always had, oblivious to the danger that thrives in the city right beneath your nose. And for a while I thought I could make it work, but when your place got broken in to, I knew I'd been living a lie and I couldn't subject you to further harm."

"You could've trusted me and given me a chance to make the choice whether I wanted to stay or go. Instead you didn't give me any options and simply did things your way, and look how everything has crumbled around you."

"It's not a question of trusting you. Don't you realize you deserve to have better?"

"Damn you, Nathan. It's not your job to determine what I deserve. It's my choice the way I live my life or who I allow in it."

They drove until the lights of the city began to fade and the streetlamps became less maintained and the road less smooth until they rolled into a really old, forgotten neighborhood that had fallen into disrepair. Perhaps at one time it had been posh because Jaci could see evidence of good solid craftsmanship in the sagging eaves of some of the houses and she wondered how many lives had come and gone over each threshold through the years. There was a sadness clinging to the street as a deathly quiet filled the air. She couldn't stop the shudder that followed as she said, "It's kind of creepy. Now I know why no one wants to stay here."

Nathan agreed as he climbed from the truck. "Yeah, it's no five star, that's for sure. But that suits our purposes perfectly. The less people snooping around, the better."

Jaci followed Nathan as they walked up to the old, still house, it's darkened shutters not the least bit inviting for any length of time and Jaci asked, "Is there even electricity or running water?"

"I hope so. Only one way to find out."

"Did I ever tell you I've never been a fan of camping?" she muttered and Nathan actually chuckled under his breath. The house looked like a hiding point for every refugee of the wildlife kingdom and some of the insect world, too, and Jaci wondered for a brief moment if staying alive was worth the price of staying one moment in that house.

Talk about your low-rent accommodations, he thought grimly to himself as they carefully navigated the dark house in search of a light switch or flashlight to see by. He banged his shin several times on various hard lumps of furniture and by the time his questing fingers found a small lamp by the decrepit sofa, his legs were throbbing from each hit. He held his breath and snapped on the light. To his relief it popped on, shedding a watery glow on the dismal surroundings. Something scurried from the weak illumination and Jaci jumped, stuffing her fist in her mouth to keep from shrieking. "Most likely a rat," he said with a grimace. "Stay here while I do a quick search and make sure there's nothing else hiding in the corners." Nathan pulled his gun and motioned for Jaci to stay put while he secured the house.

The tight quarters left little to hide, probably one of the reasons ID had purchased the house back in the Stone Age as the house had little by way of convenience. Frankly he was almost surprised it had an indoor toilet. There was one double bed in the master bedroom that looked as appealing as a bed of nails and another bedroom off to the left that housed a sagging twin bed, the mattress likely a home for a host of vermin.

He returned to find Jaci in the same spot he'd left

her, her expression leaving no room for confusion as to her feelings about the place. "Sorry," he said with a sigh. "It sucks but at least we're safe. The windows are bulletproof glass and the doors have reinforced locks with steel frames. Anyone trying to get at us from outside is going to give us fair enough warning so we can bug out before they succeed." He was trying to make her feel safe but she still looked miserable. He went to the sofa and jerked the covering free to shake out the dust and then replaced it, saying as he tried to make the best of it, "The place isn't that bad when you get over the shock. I mean, it's not luxury but with a little bit of elbow grease, it could be a decent place to hole up."

She shot him an incredulous look before gingerly sitting on the sofa. "This is worse than camping," she said. "At least when you're camping, you have s'mores to eat."

He laughed and sat beside her, drawing her close when she looked ready to burst into tears. "Camping can be fun," he said, telling himself he was just trying to ease her fear and take her mind off the situation for at least a moment but as soon as she leaned into him, he wanted to tip her head toward him to seal his mouth to hers. "The good news is, there aren't many things around that can actually kill you, bug- or reptile-wise. Unlike when I was stationed in Afghanistan where the hobo spider or brown recluse can really wreck your life."

"What about black widows?" she reminded him.

"James got bitten by a widow when he was clearing out the garage and he had to go to the hospital."

Nathan gritted his teeth at the mention of her hero, James, knowing his reaction was off base. But it was hard to reconcile the fact that another man had been there for her when he could not. And because he couldn't simply let it go, he asked in the most casual tone he could muster, "I don't remember you mentioning James when we were dating.... How long have you known each other?"

"We've been friends for years," she answered, oblivious to his churning jealousy. "We went to school together but we sort of drifted apart—you know how it happens when life simply takes you in different directions. But he really came through for me when I needed him. He didn't hesitate to offer me a place to stay when I called him crying. He's a very good friend."

"Yeah, I can imagine," he said, not buying James's seeming benevolence without ulterior motives. "You don't think that maybe James has a thing for you? Seems a perfect scenario if you ask me. Vulnerable girl in a bad situation, the guy rides in like the hero and saves the day."

She pulled away, a frown creasing her forehead. "That's not what happened. James is a friend and only a friend. I can guarantee he's never looked at me in that way."

"I beg to differ. He seemed pretty protective of you that day in the library."

"As a friend."

"As a potential love interest," he corrected her.

Her frown smoothed out and she said coolly, "Well, either way, I don't see how it's any of your business. We're not dating and the whole reason I needed a place to stay was because you had duped me into thinking I was going to be living with you in a beautiful house with a gorgeous backyard up in the hills. So...shut it and leave it be."

Everything she said was true. But he still wanted to push the venerable James off a pier. It was dumb caveman mentality but unlike Jaci, he wasn't naive to the way James had looked at her. Whether she realized it or not, James was hoping to become more than a just a friend.

And sorry, James...that just wasn't going to happen—not if Nathan had anything to do with it.

"I'm just saying not everyone plays their ace the minute the game starts," he said.

At that Jaci held his stare and he felt skinned to his bones as she said, "Yes, I've figured that out, thanks to you. If you're finished being a hypocrite, I'd like to get back to the business of staying alive. You were right. Talking about the past is a dead-end street." She rose and dusted off her behind. "I need to find a bathroom."

"Second door on the right," he muttered, angry at himself for venturing into territory that was off-limits for good reason. He *was* being a hypocrite but he couldn't help himself.

With Jaci he always lost control of everything...including his heart.

Chapter 14

James startled as he opened the front door and saw Jaci and Nathan sitting in his living room waiting for him. Jaci jumped up and wrapped her friend in a tight hug. "Why don't you answer your phone? You had us worried sick that something terrible had happened to you," she admonished with equal parts exasperation and relief that he was okay.

James, looking as if he'd been pulling several all-nighters with the help of street drugs and coffee, ran a hand through his grimy hair and mumbled an apology as he flopped into his desk chair where his computer was working on some task. Jaci watched the rapidly scrolling numbers on the screen and asked, "Did you find a way into the database?"

"Sort of." He cast a look at Nathan. "It's not as if I can just use a standard hack for this kind of stuff. Backdoor channels all the way and even still, it's pretty slow. Plus, there's the whole not-wanting-to-die thing that's tripping me up."

"I'm sorry, James, that I put you in this position," she said, feeling terrible. "I didn't know who else to ask."

"It's okay," he said. "For you, the risk is worth it."

Jaci caught Nathan's subtle eye roll and she tried to forget what Nathan had said about James's feelings for her. "What did you find?" she asked.

"I managed to find a backdoor channel to an older email service provider, which then allowed me into the current email settings and accounts." As Jaci and Nathan started to get excited, James shut them down fairly quickly. "But here's the catch…it's all in binary code. It would take weeks to unravel all the data and something tells me you don't have weeks for me to do this."

Jaci moaned with disappointment. "No, we don't have weeks," she answered, looking to Nathan. "Now what?"

Nathan took a long moment to think and then said, "What if you could log in with my email account into the system? Would that give you any kind of advantage?"

"Do you have administrative privileges on the system?" James asked wryly to which Nathan shook his head. "Then no. But if you could get a password with admin privies then I could easily get in, select the files you need and back out again relatively undetected."

"Do you know who might have admin privileges?" she asked Nathan.

"Tom," he answered with certainty. "He's at the top of the food chain and has all-access clearance to every op in ID."

"And I doubt he's going to hand over his password just to be helpful," she murmured. "We're screwed."

James leaned forward and rubbed his eyes free of something and when he refocused his red-shot eyes, Jaci felt an admonishment on the tip of her tongue for not taking care of himself but she held it in check for Nathan's sake. She shouldn't give a damn what Nathan thought about the people in her personal life but for some reason it mattered to her what he construed about her relationship with James. She forced a warm smile in spite of the disappointment, saying. "Thank you, James, for trying. We set you on an impossible task to begin with. Don't feel bad that you didn't succeed."

"I just need more time," James countered with frustration. "Their system is tough but not so tough that I couldn't crack it with a little more time."

"Sadly, that's the one thing we can't give you," she said, looking to Nathan who nodded in agreement. "Besides, I don't want you to get in any deeper. This is dangerous stuff. I don't want you to get hurt."

James smiled blearily at her worry and Jaci nearly smacked him for not being serious when he said, "This is the most fun I've had in ages. It's been a long time since I'd encountered anything resembling a challenge. I'm not giving up yet," he added with a renewed vigor that she didn't think was possible. "I'm just hitting my stride. A few more double espressos and I'll be attaining the subspace of my true hacker abilities."

"Okay, now I know you're delirious. Please get some sleep and eat some real food," she advised him with true worry. "I'm serious, James."

"Let the man do his work," Nathan said to Jaci, giving James a nod of approval. "If he says he's close, let's give him the space to make it happen. We can give you twenty-four hours. Will that work?"

"I'll take it," James said. "Now get out of here before I lose my steam."

Jaci didn't want to leave but Nathan seemed more than happy to watch James melt his brain on this foolhardy mission. She glared up at Nathan as he hustled her out of the apartment but she waited until they were back in the truck to let him have it. "You are something else, you know that?" she said.

"What are you talking about?"

"Don't play innocent with me, Nathan. You know that James isn't going to be able to break into the database and yet you encouraged him to keep at it. Did you not see how terrible he looked?"

"He looked like warmed-over dog crap," he agreed without hesitation but added to her surprise, "But genius is one step from crazy and since he's plainly tipping over into mental status, I figure the answer to our problems isn't far behind. Sometimes you have to let the crazy out to truly see the genius emerge."

"What? That's...ridiculous," she stated until she really gave his theory more thought. It was true that she'd never seen James so laser focused before. In fact, in the past James was always more chill and laid-back—almost lazy—about most things, but a fire had been burning behind his eyes that she'd never seen before, which made her wonder if Nathan was right. "How do you know this?"

"I've worked with a few geniuses in my time. Their hardwiring is different from ours but about the same with each other. I say all James needs is another twenty-four hours and either his brain will explode with an aneurysm—" she gasped and he continued with a shrug "—or he'll get us the information we need. So, we have twenty-four hours to kill until then. Cabin or safe house?"

She shuddered at the thought of spending another moment in that decrepit architectural relic and in spite of the long drive, answered almost gratefully, "Cabin."

Jaci fell asleep during the ride back to the cabin and Nathan used the quiet time as an opportunity to sort through the tangle of questions that had been pestering him since he'd talked to Miko.

He knew that if he didn't figure out who was behind all of this he'd likely spend the rest of his life looking over his shoulder, just as Miko was. And that was no life at all.

The fact of the matter was, if Miko didn't skip town, whoever was after him would eventually get Miko, too, no matter how many thugs he employed. No one was invulnerable forever. Eventually the targets always let their guard down and they received a bullet sandwich for their trouble.

How did things get so screwed up? When he first started with ID, he knew that he was doing his country a service, taking down the bad guys. He didn't need to be a hero but he'd be a liar if he didn't admit that he liked knowing he was on the right side. But now? If it turned out that he'd been working for the wrong side all along, he wasn't sure how to handle that turn of events.

Jaci stirred in her sleep, making a small noise of protest as if being pursued by invisible attackers and he couldn't help but smile. Jaci had always been a restless sleeper. The first time that he'd heard her talk in her sleep, she'd actually sounded coherent. It wasn't until he realized there was no way she could be asking him to go buy bunion cream to put on her bagel that he surmised that she was talking in her sleep. Honestly, it may have been weird to admit but he found her sleeping habits pretty endearing. It was part of what made her special and unique as well as made sleeping with her an adventure.

By the time they reached the cabin it was nearly three in the morning and there was no waking her. He picked her up gently and carried her into the house. He got to the living room and was headed for the bedroom when she stirred and looked at him blearily. “What are you doing? And why are you carrying me?”

“You were sleeping. I didn’t want to wake you.”

She gave him a sleepy smile but insisted that she could walk. “You’re going to kaleidoscope your spine.” But as he put her down, she surprised him when she held out her hand. “It’s late. Let’s go to bed.”

He should have said no. He should have taken his place on the guest bed but he was tired and the thought of sleeping alone after everything they’d learned tonight didn’t appeal at all. “Are you sure?” he asked, holding his breath and praying she didn’t change her mind.

“I wouldn’t ask if I wasn’t.” And then she pulled him toward the bedroom and he followed without another word.

Chapter 15

Jaci awoke from a frightening dream and burrowed more tightly into the warm body beside her. She felt surrounded by solid strength and when her eyes slowly opened to the early dawn she realized it was Nathan she was snuggled up to. His arms tightened instinctually around her and she sighed with happiness. She'd missed this.

She was embarrassed to admit that she'd wrapped a body pillow with one of his old T-shirts that he'd left behind and often snuggled with it if only to pretend that he hadn't gone away. So much had been revealed in such a short amount of time that her mind was still spinning with all the information. But the one thing that stood out clearly against the noise was that Nathan had never stopped loving her. Nathan, in his mixed up logic, had left her so that he could protect her. To her the idea of purposefully breaking someone's heart to protect them seemed bonkers. But she supposed to a man, whose thinking was always a little off center anyway, perhaps it made some sense.

Another thing that was very clear to her was even though he might admit that he still cared for her, he had every intention of setting her free. More of his misguided attempts at protecting her, she thought wryly. She hadn't realized that she seemed like such a weak, vulnerable little lamb that everyone had to go out of their way to protect her. Frankly she found this a little mortifying. She'd always pictured herself as a take-charge, modern woman who could handle any obstacle. Clearly she was the only one who saw herself in this way.

Somehow she had to convince him that they were meant to be together. And when all of this nasty business was finished and figured out, she wanted him to realize that they were a good match and that he was the only one for her. Of course, there were two obstacles to her plan. One, they might not live to see tomorrow; two, Nathan was notoriously stubborn and it would take a stick of dynamite to dislodge his caveman idea of setting her free to keep her safe.

Well, she wasn't afraid of a challenge. And she was willing to use all the tools in her arsenal to get her way, which included, but weren't limited to, hitting below the belt—or more specifically *touching* below the belt.

* * *

Nathan awoke as if swimming to the surface of a deep lake. Each stroke brought him closer to air but it was a slog to reach the top. However, as he slowly came to, his eyes fluttered shut again as a groan escaped his mouth when the wet and wonderful sensation of a mouth descending on a very sensitive part of his body jolted him into complete awareness of what was happening and who was doing it to him.

His hands threaded through Jaci's thick hair and he caressed her scalp as she pleasured him with sure and steady strokes that both teased and tantalized, nearly causing his hips to thrust from the bed. Her name slipped from his lips as he urged her to seat herself on his length but she continued to torture him with her sweet mouth until he was afraid he might lose himself prematurely. She seemed to sense he was close and she straddled him, sinking onto his straining length, her head tipped back in ecstasy, lifting her beautiful breasts so that the pink-tipped nipples jutted proudly as if begging for his caress. He quickly filled his palms with what she was offering and rose up to slip a pebbled nipple into his greedy mouth as she wrapped her legs around his torso.

They moved together in slow, rhythmic tandem, taking and giving from one another until he rolled her to her back and rose above her, gazing down at her and drinking in every detail of her face and committing it to memory.

She smoothed his hair from his face and met his

stare with soft, lust-filled eyes to murmur, "I've missed you so much, Nathan..." and his heart cracked in two at the honest sentiment. He couldn't tell her how much he'd wanted to touch her, to sleep beside her one more time and go back just one more day so he could pretend that a life together was possible. She knew the score—this was temporary—but oh, he'd give his soul to keep this time forever and hold it close to his heart.

He captured her mouth and thrust deeper inside her wet heat, loving the way she gasped and shook as if she couldn't quite possibly contain the pleasure rolling through her. He thrust harder and faster, hitting the sweet spot deep inside her the way he knew drove her crazy and within moments, she was crying out, clutching at his back as he pushed her to the tipping point and straight over into sweet oblivion. She shuddered and cried, her breathy moans the catalyst to his final release. Nathan lost himself in her folds until he collapsed, completely spent.

His heart beat frantically as he tried to recover but he felt as if he'd run a marathon. Sweat trickled down his temples and his body was slick with moisture. He threw his arm over his eyes and willed his breathing to return to normal. Suddenly he realized Jaci was watching him, her eyes damp. "What's wrong?" he asked, alarmed. "Did I hurt you?"

She shook her head and leaned over to kiss him. "Tell me you love me," she instructed in a sweet, feather-soft voice. It was a simple request, one he could easily accomplish because it was true. But he knew if he said the words, the dynamic would change between them and he couldn't take the risk with her safety. Pushing away the sweetness of their lovemaking, he rolled until he was sitting up, casting her a warning look. "I'm going to hit the shower," he said, expecting her to appear wounded at his deflection but instead, he saw determination and that scared him more than the idea of her tears.

"Jaci…whatever you're thinking, stop," he demanded in a stern voice but she ignored him and sauntered past—her gloriously naked body made him hard with fresh desire and she knew it. "Jaci, I know what you're doing and it's not going to work…"

"I don't know what you're talking about," she said, bending over to start the water, treating him to a lovely view. He groaned silently and followed her into the bathroom, shutting the door with his foot. She glanced coyly over her shoulder, a secret smile twisting her lips. "Care to join me in the shower?" she asked in a sultry voice that did terrible things to his resolve.

"Wench, you'll be the death of us both," he bit out before sealing his mouth to hers again, pushing her against the door. She laughed in open delight at his domination but grabbed a handful of his man parts, reminding him that she had ways of bringing him to his knees. And now that he thought of it—he sank to his knees and buried his face in her feminine place, loving every second of this blissful torture. Reality would come soon enough.… Besides, if he were going to face death, he couldn't think of a better memory to take with him.

Finished with the shower and towel drying her hair, Jaci felt light and happy from the inside out. If crazy people were determined to snuff out their lights, she'd say the time spent at the cabin with Nathan was near perfect. Okay, well, the sex was perfect. They had always been well tuned in that department. Their first month together had been a dizzying circus of intense, passionate sex where they'd practically hung from the ceiling in their wild abandon.

She sighed at the memory but realized as amazing as that first month had been, nothing compared to the sex they'd just enjoyed. Talk about explosive. The heat in the room could've melted the fixtures. When things settled down, they'd have to return to the cabin to make some new memories—ones not contaminated by the whole "running for their lives and hiding from killers" thing.

"I'm starved. How about I see what's in the kitchen that I can whip up?" she suggested as Nathan pulled his jeans on.

"I'll meet you down there," he said, giving her a rare smile that delighted her to her toes.

She fairly skipped to the kitchen and was amazed at how light she felt on her feet. Before she knew it, she began humming beneath her breath to the tune of "I Want Your Sex" by George Michael—that song had always felt so decadently naughty in her opinion—and she was feeling positively sinful as she bounced into the kitchen to throw open the fridge to survey the contents. She grabbed a few eggs and spun around in her own world to find a bowl when she felt something hard and distinctly gun muzzle-ish pressing into her spine at the same time that her head was wrenched back in a painful viselike grip. She choked back a scream as the gun pressed harder into skin and her suddenly nerveless fingers dropped the eggs to splatter in a mess all over the floor, fear hammering away the remnants of all her good feelings. "Call your boyfriend," a voice whispered in her ear.

"No." She gasped at the pain centered at her scalp and radiating through her head. "Go screw yourself!"

"Call him or I'll make you watch him die," the voice warned, his breath hot against her ear. She pressed her lips together and his grip tightened on her hair. "I bet you're a hot lay. Maybe I'll sample the goods a little before I put a bullet in your brain. Would you like that?"

Nathan called out from upstairs, "You okay?" he asked. "I'll be right down to help. I think there's some cheese in the fridge for omelets…"

No, Nathan, don't come downstairs…. Tears stung her eyes as she thought frantically what to do. *Think!* But fear and adrenaline had mixed together and caused her muscles to freeze. As much as she wanted to do something brave and spectacular, she simply couldn't compel herself to do much more than shake in her captor's grip with tears leaking down her face at her own failure to save herself or Nathan. She didn't want to die.... She squeezed her eyes shut and whimpered. Hopefully, it would be quick.

Chapter 16

Nathan stilled when Jaci didn't answer. There was an unnatural quiet in the cabin that put Nathan's nerves on edge. Jaci was notoriously loud in the kitchen. There should have been the sound of pots and pans clanging, her dropping things and possibly her singing off tune. The ensuing silence told him they weren't alone.

He cursed himself for being sloppy when he realized his gun was downstairs. He glanced around, quickly looking for something that could serve as a weapon. He crossed to the closet and slid it open quietly. After tossing aside a few articles of clothing he had hanging on the rod, he unscrewed the wooden dowel and hefted it in his hand, testing the weight. It was better than nothing.

"Hey, Jase, did you find the cheese?" He called out, modulating his voice to make it sound as if he were none the wiser.

"Yes." She answered with a subtle strain to her tone, the slightest tremor beneath the single word confirmed his suspicion. Someone had discovered their hideout.

Nathan considered his options. If he went down the hall he would have no element of surprise, which was a tremendous loss considering he didn't have his gun. If he climbed out the window and tried to come in behind the attacker he might waste precious time that Jaci didn't have. In the end the decision was made for him.

"Your girlfriend is not very cooperative," a male voice called out, causing Nathan's muscles to tense. Was Jaci hurt? Was he too late to save her? There was only one way to find out.

Nathan walked into the hall and the kitchen came into view. The tall, lean man with hard features had his hand twisted tightly in Jaci's beautiful red hair and a gun muzzle pressed into the small of her back. Nathan swallowed the rage that rose to the surface when he saw Jaci being abused. The man smiled with derision at the wooden dowel in Nathan's hand and said, "And what do you plan to do with that? Bash my head in?"

Nathan smiled. "The thought had crossed my mind."

The man's gaze narrowed and he jerked his head as he said, "Toss it over there. I rather like my head the way it is. You know, you're a hard man to find. I was forced to follow your ISP to find where you are logging in to get your emails. Otherwise, I might never have found this piece of shit cabin in the middle of nowhere."

Nathan cursed himself for being a clumsy fool. He should've known an ISP would betray his location. He tossed the dowel and it clattered on the hard floor, rolling away. "Now what? You have me at a disadvantage but I suspect that's the way you prefer it because otherwise I would kill you."

"Yes, perhaps. Here's what is going to happen. You're going to tell me all the people you've talked to about the kill order you weren't supposed to see and then I'm going to bury a bullet in your brain along with your girlfriend and then walk away and leave your corpses here to rot."

Jaci whimpered and Nathan retorted, "Now, that doesn't sound very appealing to me. How about you let the girl go and we settle this man-to-man."

"And why would I do that?"

"Integrity?"

The man laughed. "Who knew you had such a great sense of humor?" he said but his smile faded soon enough. His gaze dipped down to Jaci's cleavage and lingered as he said, "She's a fine piece of ass. If you tell me what I want to know, I won't defile her body before putting a bullet in her pretty head. Your choice."

"If you touch her, I will kill you slowly," Nathan promised. "Better men than you have tried to kill me and I'm still here. What does that say about your chances?"

The man didn't seem the least bit frightened by Nathan's stark promise. Nathan edged forward, his gaze never leaving the man's. There was something about the man's lean build that sparked a memory. "You're the one who broke into Jaci's apartment a couple of months ago."

The man nodded.

"You ran away like a coward before I could finish you off, but I'm more than happy to complete what I started. You made a big mistake coming back for more. You should've kept running."

"I didn't run. I simply reevaluated my position. A smart man never lets his head overrule good tactical sense."

"Agreed," Nathan said in a hard tone. "But a smart man also knows when he's outmatched. You, obviously, have no sense of self-preservation."

"Life is fleeting," the man said with a shrug as he leaned toward Jaci's neck and inhaled the unique scent of her skin. "Mmm…she smells like cookies. Does she taste as sweet?" He ran his tongue along her flesh and Nathan saw red but managed to keep steady. "You know, I watched her place for weeks. You weren't supposed to be there. I'd planned a fun evening of slap and tickle, or as I like to call it, slap and scream, but you ruined my plans. I've been waiting for a rain check on that night."

"As have I."

Quick as a snake the man lifted the gun and fired a shot, which tore through Nathan's biceps but missed vital organs. Jaci screamed and jammed her elbow into the man's solar plexus, giving Nathan just enough time to sprint across the living room and barrel into the man, knocking him to the floor. Blood poured from the ripped muscle but Nathan didn't feel any pain as he had one objective in mind: killing the man who'd dared to lift a finger to his girl.

They grappled on the floor, the sounds of their grunts filling the room as they scrambled and pushed and shoved and kicked and punched as each tried to gain the upper hand. Nathan smashed his elbow into the man's nose, shattering it, but that didn't slow him down. The man countered with a knee to the groin causing Nathan to grunt and see stars but he knew he couldn't give in to the agony or the fact that he couldn't breathe because if he did the bastard would kill them both. He pushed past the dull, aching throb in his junk and landed another hit to the man's jaw just as he was reaching for the gun that had skittered from his fingers.

In a swift move that shocked him, Jaci smashed their attacker in the head with a frying pan, knocking him out cold. Nathan stared up at his girl with open surprise and more than a little pride. Breathing heavily he got to his feet and offered her a grin. "Good job," he said, staring down at the man. "Help me drag him into the living room."

Jaci stared and dropped the frying pan as tears welled up in her eyes. "Did I kill him? Oh, God, please say that I didn't kill him."

So tenderhearted. "No, you didn't kill him. But when he wakes up he's going to have one heck of a headache." He picked up the man's feet and gestured for her to do the same with his hands. "I need to ask him some questions and his answers will determine whether he lives or dies."

"You're going to kill him?" Jaci looked appalled. "That makes you no better than him. And if you kill him won't that be messy? There will be blood everywhere." She put a hand to her mouth. "I think I'm going to be sick."

"Jaci, focus." They dragged the man over to the sofa and dumped him on it. Nathan secured his hands and feet with plenty of rope and once their attacker was trussed safely Jaci realized that Nathan was bleeding.

"Oh, my God! You've been shot!" Jaci dragged him over to the sink and began to gingerly wipe the wound with a wet washcloth. "We need to get you to a hospital," she said, her brow furrowing with concern. "I can't believe you were shot and you still fought him. What are you, a superhero?"

He tried not to put too much stock in her praise but he had to admit it felt good. "It's not that bad," he said gruffly. "Trust me, I've had worse."

"Worse? Wonderful. I forgot in your line of work people shoot at you."

"Actually, I'm usually the one doing the shooting. But when I served in Iraq my unit got caught in some rebel cross fire and I ended up taking a bullet to the leg. Nearly bled out before they could get me to a medic. So this?" He gestured to his shoulder. "Is nothing. We can douse it with antiseptic and butterfly it shut and it'll be fine."

She didn't look convinced. "Are you sure?" she asked, and he loved her for it.

"I'm sure." And because he couldn't help himself, he pulled her in for a quick kiss. She softened beneath his touch and when he pulled away she had lost some of the fear in her eyes. "See? I'm fine."

She nodded and drew a halting breath as her gaze strayed to the destroyed kitchen where bits of broken eggs littered the floor along with several glasses and plates that'd been knocked over during the fight. "I'm going to clean up the mess," she said and Nathan knew she needed to regroup to process what had just happened. She stopped and turned suddenly. "Please don't kill him in the living room." The pleading in her eyes softened his stance and he nodded in agreement. She offered a brief smile in thanks and then began to wipe up the eggs and shattered kitchenware.

An hour later the man began to stir and Nathan tossed a glass of water in his face. He came to with a quick sputter and a glare reserved for Nathan as he hunkered down to stare him in the eye. "You're going to tell me who sent you or I'm going to make giving you pain my new favorite game," Nathan said.

"You've been in this business long enough to know that the people who hire us don't appreciate tattletales. I'm dead either way."

"Yes, but there's dead and then there's *dead.* What matters is how you arrive at that final destination. I can offer you the same deal you offered me—tell me what I want to know and I'll make it quick and painless. Jerk me around and I'll make you wish you were never born."

"Tempting, but I prefer to be the master of my own fate." The man's grim smile puzzled Nathan until a second later; the man's jaw worked and he clamped down hard on something inside his mouth.

Nathan jumped back and stared in frustration as the man began to convulse as the poison caplet, which had been inside his tooth filling, did its job of killing him.

Jaci came skidding into the living room, her eyes wide with horror. "What happened?" she asked.

"Cyanide caplet. I should've known," he said, irritated. "Now he's useless to me."

"Now there's a dead guy in the living room!" Jaci shrieked. "A dead guy. A *freaking* dead guy! What are you going to do with him?"

"I'll dump his body deep in the woods. The critters will eat him." At her mortified and disgusted expression, he added, "Trust me, that's better than this piece of crap deserves. Make no mistake, he was going to kill us both but he would've done worse to you. I saw the look in his eyes and what he wanted. Frankly, he's lucky he took the easy way out."

Her eyes watered and he didn't understand why she was crying over a bastard who'd wanted them both dead. "Don't waste your tears over this guy," he said sharply, which earned him a dark look from Jaci as she wiped at her eyes and stalked from the kitchen.

"What?" he asked, wanting to follow her but knowing he didn't have time. Pretty soon this corpse was going to start leaking and he did not want to deal with that. He hefted the body over his shoulder and left the cabin. He tossed the body in the back of his truck and fired up the engine. Would he ever understand that woman? Likely not. He sighed and rumbled down the driveway to find a good, secluded place to dump a body.

She wasn't crying because the man was dead but because she'd been so useless in the fight. Sure, she'd hit the guy with a frying pan but not before nearly peeing herself in the beginning. When she'd felt the muzzle pressing into her back, her brain had frozen. Why hadn't she tried to jam her elbow in his solar plexus or stomped on his instep? She'd taken a self-defense class once and yet, in the heat of the moment, she'd done nothing but shake in fear. How could she explain to Nathan that she was embarrassed for being a hindrance rather than an ally in that fight? How could she possibly consider herself a strong woman when she'd acted like a ninny back there?

Her shoulders shook as tears coursed down her cheeks. Shock was setting in. She'd watched a man die. Her stomach cramped. The memory of Sonia dying right in front of her came back to haunt her. She could smell the sizzling flesh; she could see her best friend's sightless eyes as she'd crumpled to the dirty pavement. Jaci ground her fists into her eyes as if she could wipe away the memory with the heel of her palm but there was no ridding herself of what was stuck in her head.

She'd been stupid and naive to allow herself to think that when this was all over they'd still be alive. Two hours ago she'd been blissfully happy, floating on a cloud of sexual satisfaction, completely glossing over the fact that they were on the run and that someone really bad wanted them both dead. Now nothing felt safe.

Nathan had been shot—what if the bullet had pierced his heart? Dodging bullets might be commonplace for Nathan, but for her it was a shocking event. And if that man hadn't killed himself, Nathan would have done the job for him. Nathan had tried to tell her that he was a killer but for some reason the cold hard fact hadn't completely registered in her brain. Coming face-to-face with the knowledge that Nathan took other people's lives for a living suddenly smacked her in the nose. She hadn't realized how long she'd been sitting on the bed staring at her fingers until Nathan returned and found her sitting that way. "Are you okay?" he asked.

She looked up at him. "Am I okay?" she repeated, her voice rising. "No, I'm not okay. I didn't ask for this. I'm a graphic designer, not a spy. I shop at IKEA because I like the cafeteria but not so much that you have to use their warehouse to find the items you want to buy and I always thought that someday I would meet a guy I would want to marry and have kids with but never imagined that that man would be someone who kills people for a living."

"Don't fall apart on me now, Jaci," Nathan warned.

"I need you to focus. The cabin isn't safe anymore. We have to leave."

"And go where? This was your safe house! This was the place that no one could find! Where do you suggest we go? The moon?"

"I don't know. But for the time being we will go back to the safe house on the edge of the city. No one will think to look for us there."

"That's because no one in their right mind would stay there."

He shrugged. "Whatever it takes. If it means staying in the worst place on this planet to keep you safe, I'm willing to do that. Staying alive is what's important."

She buried her face in her hands and cried openly. She wasn't cut out for this. "I was so scared," she admitted with a hiccup. "I tried to move but I was paralyzed with fear. He thought I wasn't being cooperative because I wouldn't call you downstairs but the truth of the matter was I couldn't get my vocal cords to work. I wasn't being sly or deliberately difficult, just scared silly."

Nathan heard the mortification in her voice and came to sit beside her, pulling her into his arms. She went willingly and sobbed against his shirt. "You were great back there," he murmured. "No one knows how they will react in a crisis. But you did exactly the right thing."

"You're just saying that so I don't feel so pathetic," she said with a watery sniff. "But it's not working because I know how pathetic I was. I want to be a kick-ass woman so you don't have to constantly worry about me being in danger. But I wasn't kick-ass at all. I was weak and stupid and…I don't know, not very brave!"

"You hit him with a frying pan," he reminded her. "That took balls!"

She wiped her running nose and looked up at him. "It was the only thing I could think of to hit him with," she admitted, adding morosely. "I should've grabbed the gun."

He surprised her by hooking her chin with his knuckles and forcing her to hold his stare. "Listen to me—I would never want you to suffer under the guilt that follows when you take a life, no matter how vile that life was. I would gladly bear that burden so you never have to." Tears continued to stream down her face and his lips twisted in a subtle smile as he said, "Has anyone ever told you that you're cute even when you're crying?"

She laughed at that ridiculous question and knew he was just trying to distract her from the horror of what had just happened but she loved him for it. "Next gunfight, I will totally kick ass," she promised with a tremulous smile.

He kissed her and said, "I know you will."

She burrowed into his embrace and squeezed her eyes shut, knowing what he didn't say.

The next gunfight, neither might survive.

Chapter 17

For the first time ever Nathan didn't have a plan of action. With his assignments, the objective had been clear and he'd always set out with a clear plan but now, he had no idea which way to turn. And the fact that he had Jaci tagging along only made the pressure that much greater.

"I'm going to set you up in the safe house and then I'm going to go to ID alone," he said as they drove. Her alarmed expression was expected but he pushed forward in spite of her immediate protests. "They aren't expecting me to walk through the front doors. We need an admin password and the only way I know how to get one is through ID."

"I think that's a terrible idea," Jaci countered hotly.

"Even if they aren't expecting you to walk through the front door, wouldn't that be like having their quarry tied up nice and neat with a bow? And furthermore, you're not leaving me in that haunted house with nothing more than the rats for company, so think again."

"It's not up for discussion. If I walk in there with you, they'll know something is up. I'm banking on the fact that whoever is after me doesn't realize that I know about this latest attempt. Besides, I need to talk to Tom. If he's behind the hit I want to see it in his eyes."

"Stop with the macho bullshit. I don't want you doing anything that can get you killed and walking up to the man we *suspect* is behind all of this is just plain stupid."

"You don't know Tom like I do. He was there for me when no one else was."

"You're still hanging on to the hope that he's innocent," she said, shaking her head. "If the shoe were on the other foot and I kept clinging to the hope that someone who obviously looked guilty was actually innocent, what would you say to me?"

"I'd say you're being stupid," he agreed. "And maybe I am being reckless but I have to know."

Tom had been like a father to him over the years. It hurt to even think that Tom might have something to do with the plot to kill him but if Tom was guilty, Nathan was going to make him look him in the eye before he killed him. "It's just something I have to do. I'm sorry you don't understand."

"And just like that, discussion closed. Damn you

Nathan, this is what I was talking about—you can't just make arbitrary decisions that affect the both of us. What's going to happen if you die and I'm left sitting in that moldering house? Am I supposed to just sit there like a lump until someone else comes along and finishes me off?"

He didn't have an answer for her and the fact was he didn't have anything that he could say that would justify his actions in her eyes. And he didn't want to try. "Have you heard from James?" he asked, changing the subject. She glowered at him but shook her head. "Call him on the burner and let him know we're on our way."

She nodded sullenly but otherwise remained quiet as she dialed her friend's number. After a few rings she hung up. "Voice mail."

Seeing as he hadn't answered his phone the last time they called, Nathan wasn't too worried. Either the man had suffered an aneurysm or he was simply too engrossed in his work to bother with the phone—hopefully it was the latter. He'd hate to have another one of Jaci's friends go down because of all this. But the stark truth was Nathan was willing to sacrifice every single one of her friends if it meant she remained safe. Of course he valued his nuts so he kept that sentiment to himself.

Jaci knew that Nathan was trying to protect her. And given everything that had happened in the past few hours, she didn't blame him for being overprotective. If the situation were reversed, she'd probably feel compelled to do the same but as much as he wanted to protect her, the idea of something bad happening to Nathan made her blood run cold. There had to be something she could do to help. "So what's your plan?" she asked, trying to seem as if she were on board. "Just walk in with a smile?"

"Pretty much. I figure I need to act as normal as possible."

"Have you contacted Tom through all of this?"

"Once. I sent him a quick email and told him I'd be in touch."

"So you didn't give him any details on what was going on?"

"No."

She let that information sink into her brain for a second and then said, "So as far as anyone at the office is concerned, you're just taking a few days off. Right?" At Nathan's nod, she continued, "And no one knows about me and Sonia in the alley because only Sonia was found by the police, right?"

"Yeah. What are you getting at?"

"I think we should walk in together as a couple." She let the bomb drop and as expected, he balked. He sputtered and shook his head but she pushed forward in spite of his reaction. "Hear me out. They aren't expecting you to walk in, happy and acting like nothing's wrong. It could give you an advantage because if they sense you're on the defensive, they're going to step up their game. You need to act like nothing's wrong and that the reason that you've been incommunicado is because you and I've been too busy shacked up in your little love cabin."

She held her breath and just when she thought he was going to shut her down completely, he began a slow nod. "As crazy as that sounds, the idea has merit. The only person who would know differently is the one person who has been making all of this happen. I might be able to tell from their microexpressions who the true culprit is."

She couldn't help but be impressed. "You know how to read microexpressions?"

He shrugged. "Just one of the many skills taught to me, courtesy of the U.S. government. It comes in handy when people are trying to swindle me…or kill me."

She smiled at his tiny bit of humor. "Listen, I know that I didn't rise to the occasion very well when we were attacked at the cabin and I had a mini meltdown but I can handle being your girl for the day. How about you? Can you pretend that we're blissfully in love for the sake of putting on a show?"

"Yeah, I think I can handle that."

"Good." She tried not to feel a pinch when she realized she wouldn't be acting. "So, when we stop by James's place I'll get dressed in something more appropriate and then we'll go to your headquarters…that are probably secret and underground."

He laughed. "Our headquarters are not underground. It's just an old building that looks like a bunch of accountants work there. It's really quite ugly. We don't even have any nice art on the walls."

"Well, I guess that's good. You certainly wouldn't want to advertise that you're a bunch of killers for hire."

"True. We found putting that on a business card was far more effective."

It was her turn to laugh even though her nerves were strung tight. "Okay, let's do this."

This was her chance to show him that she could handle being his girl. *For real.*

Now if only she didn't feel the need to throw up.

They arrived at James's place and Jaci used her key to open the door. Jaci locked the door behind them and startled when she saw James slumped over his keyboard. "Oh, no!" She rushed forward but Nathan prevented her from going to James until he'd determined the coast was clear. "What are you doing?" she asked.

"Stay here." Nathan wanted to make sure a trap wasn't in place before he let Jaci near her friend, if even to check if he was alive. Nathan checked his pulse and found a steady beat. He looked to Jaci. "He's fine, just passed out."

Jaci settled down with a hand on her chest in open relief. "Oh, thank God," she murmured. "I automatically thought the worst."

"Understandable considering the circumstances. He probably hasn't slept in days. Or eaten anything beyond sugarbombs." He gestured to the wrappers of candy and soda cans littered around the desk and Jaci agreed.

"James has a terrible sweet tooth on the best of days.

I can only imagine what it's like under extreme stress," she said.

"Go get changed and I'll see what I can find to rouse him." Jaci nodded and disappeared into her bedroom while Nathan went to the kitchen and rustled up food and Gatorade. He went to James and shook him on the shoulder. "Hey, no sleeping on the job. Come on, buddy, time to get up."

James came to slowly and stared blearily at Nathan as if unable to recall who he was or why he was standing in his living room. Nathan gave him a grin and clapped him harder on the shoulder. "There he is," he said, shoving some food in his face. "Eat this and drink that," he instructed and James complied in a stupor. By the time Jaci emerged from the bedroom looking fresh and flirty in a cute sundress with her hair pinned back by a saucy headband, Nathan could only stare for a moment until he remembered why they were there. He nodded in approval to Jaci but didn't trust his ability to form the appropriate words in regards to her appearance. Instead, he focused on James. "Change of plan—we're going to get to the admin password."

James rubbed his eyes. "And how are you going to manage that?" he asked chewing slowly on a peanut butter and jelly sandwich. "It's not like they hand out those things to just anyone. Getting the admin password is like getting an all-access pass to everything on the server. Who do you know that has that kind of access?"

"The one person he knows might be trying to kill

him," Jaci interjected with a frown. "So I take it you haven't had any luck?"

"Not so," James answered, with a sloppy grin. He went to wipe peanut butter from his mouth and booted up his computer. "Having the admin password would certainly have made things easier but then I realized no self-respecting hacker would want to go the easy way. I'd forgotten how much fun it was to completely lose your mind trying to gain access to some place you didn't belong. So I tapped the collective intellect of a few trusted friends and together we created a really simple but highly effective back door into your system."

"You have my attention," Nathan said, intrigued. "What do you mean?"

"Sometimes it's the most simple but eloquent execution that delivers the results you're looking for. You'd be surprised how weak some securities are, including those of the government. Sure, banks are guarded with pretty good systems—pretty much anything that deals with money is—but for something like a clandestine U.S. government agency that isn't supposed to exist…? They could really use an upgrade on their security."

"I'm listening."

"Every agency, department, organization—you name it—has someone manning the phones. And that person usually has a computer with an email address. Now that email address doesn't have access to what we need, but usually the person manning the phones isn't somebody with top clearance experience. Am I right? Who answers your phones at ID?"

"A woman named Mandi," Nathan answered. "Why?"

James followed with a sly smile as he said, "Well, Mandi fell for the easiest trick in the book and broke a cardinal rule. Never open mail from a sender you don't recognize. I simply created a virus, and packaged it in a nice and pretty e-card that once it was opened released the virus throughout the system. Now the purpose of most viruses is to install spyware to collect personal information but I'm only interested in one piece of information—an admin password."

Nathan grinned, unable to believe that this computer nerd had managed to break into a government computer so easily; but God bless him. "And were you able to get the password?"

James smiled sheepishly. "I was going to call you but I sort of passed out."

Jaci squealed and gave him a tight hug. "I knew you could do it, James. If anyone could do it I knew you would be the one. Thank you for not giving up."

James beamed beneath the warmth of Jaci's praise and swiveled his chair to Nathan. "Okay, here goes. You're going to log in as your superior and then I'll put in the admin code. If it works, we're in. If it doesn't work, we'll need to skip the country because we're screwed."

"How soon will we know if we're screwed?" Jaci asked.

James laughed nervously. "If we get locked out of the system, they're onto us and that'll be a pretty good indication that we're screwed. Y'all have passports, right?"

"That's not funny. You know I'm afraid to fly," Jaci muttered, shooting a glance at Nathan. "What? So I'm afraid to fly, big deal. I seem to remember that you aren't very fond of parrots."

Nathan shuddered at the mention of those horrible birds. "My grandmother had a parrot. It nearly bit my finger off."

"Maybe you shouldn't stick your finger inside the cage of a big talking bird," she said with a shrug.

James cleared his throat. "As fascinating as this conversation is, can we get back to the point of why we're here and what I risked my life to get?" He gestured to the keyboard and Nathan leaned forward and typed in the URL of his remote email system. He typed in Tom's login and held his breath as James typed in the admin code. The screen flashed and suddenly they were in.

"Hot damn!" James exclaimed, slapping his knee. "It worked."

"Did you have any doubt that it wouldn't?" Jaci asked, worried.

James shrugged. "It was a risk. But worth it. This is a big deal and it's going to look great on my resume."

Jaci looked horrified. "You can't tell anyone about this. Why don't you just wave a big flag saying 'Kill Me, Kill Me.'"

"Not out in the open, goofy girl. Within the hacking community. This is going to get me some serious street cred."

Nathan went to the file database and pulled his last three jobs. He frowned, disappointed. "I've seen these files. They're basically the same thing that I have access to. There has to be something different—a secret file or a directory that is located somewhere else."

James took over, his fingers moving like lightning. He searched through pages upon pages of directories, scanning for anything that might trigger something. "All secret-government-agency guys start off in the military, right?" James asked, to which Nathan nodded. "Okay so here's what I'm thinking—I think it's a fair bet that whatever we're looking for is probably filed under something that has meaning to your director. Did he have a call sign or a nickname or something that he was known for?"

Nathan thought hard, searching his memory for any snippet of conversation that he and Tom had had in the past that might reveal a clue. Suddenly he remembered something. He snapped his fingers, saying, "Operation Sundial. Back when Tom was in the Marines he did a Special Ops detail called Operation Sundial. It made him a hero. I think it earned him a purple heart."

"Let's see if we can find Operation Sundial," James said, his finger skipping over the keys quickly. He double-clicked a folder and grinned with his success. "Got it. Here it is. Operation Sundial, buried under a bunch of layers."

Damn. The evidence against Tom was growing and

it killed Nathan, but he supposed he couldn't ignore it any longer. "Look for anything with the name Winslow, Stanislaus or Chester," he instructed grimly.

At Jaci's questioning look, he explained in a low voice. "Those are the names of my last three jobs, the ones that my gut told me weren't entirely legit."

"Oh." Jaci looked bothered by his admission but didn't say anything more. She looked to James. "Find anything?"

"Yeah. Harrison Winslow." He double-clicked the file and the dossier popped up. Nathan stared at the picture of the man he'd shot cleanly through the back of the head from a distance of a thousand yards and swallowed the lump of regret. James didn't notice Nathan's discomfort but Jaci did. Nathan refused to meet her gaze. He didn't need to see in her eyes what he felt in his heart. "What does it say?" he asked brusquely.

"It says 'neutralized.'" A beat of silence followed and they all knew what that meant. James swallowed and shot a nervous glance at Jaci. "I don't really see anything that said he was a bad guy. Actually, sounded like he was doing good work. I mean, he was developing a drug that helps boost the immune systems of cancer patients. Why wouldn't the government give this guy a medal?"

"I don't know," Nathan said. "Keep searching. There has to be something in that file."

Jaci frowned and pointed. "Is that a newspaper clipping?" James double-clicked the file and the picture got bigger, showing that it was indeed a newspaper clipping. "Why would ID need a newspaper clipping reporting Winslow's business failing?"

Nathan shook his head, wishing he had the answers.

James scanned the news article, looking for clues. "It says here that the business folded after Winslow's death. That sucks. Sounds like they were helping people"

Jaci looked to Nathan, curious. "How did ID explain Winslow's death? It's not every day that pharmaceutical company owners just get shot in the head. I'm sure there's some kind of plan for the cover-up later."

Nathan nodded. "Winslow was supposed to have ties to the opium trade. Some well-placed information to the news wires provided the cover-up."

"How so?"

James shook his head at Jaci's innocence. "They lied...and the press gobbled it up. Is that about right?" he asked Nathan.

Nathan shifted on the balls of his feet, uncomfortable. "At the time it was only a partial lie. I believed my superior when he told me that Winslow was connected to the opium trade so it was entirely plausible that Winslow had gotten caught in a deal that went sour."

Jaci stared. "Plausible, yes. The truth, no. The least the government could do is own up to their kills or whatever they're called."

"Well, we don't live in a perfect world, so people lie and governments cheat and steal and lots of bad things happen to good people. Can we move on? We're still looking for answers and this isn't helping."

"I feel sick to my stomach," Jaci said in a small voice, moving away from the computer to go to the kitchen. She reached for some bottled water and then changed her mind, muttering under her breath, "Screw it. I need a beer." She grabbed an import and cracked the top to take a long slug.

Nathan didn't blame her. A beer right about now—or twenty—sounded pretty good.

"Well, one person's tragedy is another person's fortune," James noted, clicking on another news article. "It seems as soon as Winslow's company was out of the running another company picked up where they left off. And they got a pretty lucrative contract with one of the leading drug manufacturers in the United States."

Jaci joined them, sighing sadly. "Wherever there is big money, there's greed to follow."

The scent of beer hops triggered a memory buried deep in Nathan's brain. He and Tom had been sharing a beer at Tom's place and Nathan had remarked on the beauty of Tom's new boat. At the time he didn't think much of it but had been definitely jealous. He'd always wanted a cruiser like that, something luxurious yet fast. But that was way beyond his pay grade. He'd been surprised that Tom was pulling down enough coin to pay for a toy like that. Tom had grinned and said, "You have to look into the right investments, son. The future is in research and good health. Mark my words. You ought to buy stock in a company called Tessara Pharmaceutical. They're headed in the right direction."

At the time Nathan hadn't given Tom's comment

much thought. In fact, it wasn't long before the subject had changed to something completely different and the boat and Tom's advice had been forgotten. "Can you find out who owns the company that took over Winslow's research?" Nathan asked, battling a feeling of dread in his gut.

"Yeah, that ought to be easy enough. Corporation owners are listed on tax documents," James answered, typing in the search criteria for Tessara Pharmaceutical. He leaned back so Nathan could read the list of names: Carleton Abby, Penelope Granger, Ulysses Rocha. But there was only one name with any meaning to Nathan: Thomas A. Wyatt.

Chapter 18

Jaci put on a brave smile but inside her nerves were knotted in twisted tangles of discomfort. If Nathan had suffered misgivings from the start on several of his jobs, why did he go through with the assignments? She risked a glance at him as he drove to his headquarters, his expression focused. It was one thing to wrap her head around his job knowing that he was the good guy but how was she supposed to accept his job when he was simply a government thug?

She bit her lip, hating how she felt inside. She wanted to believe in Nathan—he was a good man. Why else would he sacrifice his own happiness for her safety? If he were a bad guy, he wouldn't do that, right? She rubbed her temple and Nathan caught the motion. "Are you having second thoughts?" he asked and she forced a smile.

"No." Sort of. "Just nervous, I guess."

"We're going to go in, act all lovey-dovey and then go to Tom's office. No one will think anything's amiss because I often spent time with Tom going over briefings and whatnot, so it's not out of character."

"Great." She allowed her stare to drift to the passing city streets. They were coming into the older part of the city and she was reminded of that decrepit safe house. "Boy, you weren't kidding when you said it was an ugly building," she mused when the gunmetal gray structure came into view. It definitely looked like home to the IRS or some other austere government agency who hadn't gotten the memo that it's no longer the age of Ugly And Functional Is All That Matters. Nowadays everything had to have an aesthetic value, including the government offices—except this one. "This place is depressing," she muttered as they climbed from the truck.

"Happy faces, remember? We're in love."

"Right." She forced a bright, gooey smile and linked her arm through Nathan's as they walked through the front doors. She cooed for effect. "Ohh, honey, this place is amazing. So retro," she said and Nathan choked back a laugh at her attempt at flattery for something plainly as ugly as they came.

They walked to the front desk and a woman with a frizz of blond hair with purple tips greeted them with an inquisitive smile. "We haven't seen you around the office lately," she said, her gaze going from Nathan to Jaci with obvious curiosity. "I thought maybe you took another month-long vacation or something and then I thought, man, I need whatever employee package Nathan signed up for because I only get a week's worth of vacation each year."

"Mandi, this is my fiancée, Jaci Williams," he said, introducing her to the ditzy blonde with the unfortunate hair coloring. Jaci giggled when Nathan pulled her in close for a possessive embrace.

"He's such an animal…can hardly keep his hands to himself," Jaci whispered to Mandi with a wink. "But lord knows, I love him. The caveman."

Nathan's grip tightened on her hip and she sent him a cheeky grin. She was playing it over-the-top but she didn't care. At least when she was focused on playing a part, she wasn't dwelling on the uncomfortable ethical questions swirling in her brain.

Mandi sighed. "You're so lucky. I'd give my right arm for a man like Nathan. He's one of the good ones."

"Yes, he is," Jaci agreed with an adoring smile.

"Is Tom in today?" he asked casually and Mandi bobbed her head but she appeared bothered.

"That poor man. Something is eating him in the shorts lately. You know, I would never speak out of turn because he's the most amazing boss a girl could ever ask for but he snapped at me yesterday for no good reason. Of course, I didn't hold it against him because he looked as if he hadn't slept in days, the poor thing. But it did hurt my feelings a bit. I won't lie."

"I'm sure he didn't mean anything by it. You know Tom.... He's always the first to ask you how your day is and the last to leave the office at night." He assured Mandi that all was well and Tom had probably simply been overworked, and then went to the elevator.

"Want me to tell him you're on your way up?" Mandi asked helpfully as she lifted the phone receiver, but Nathan shook his head.

"I want to surprise him," he answered, putting his finger up to his pursed lips, and Mandi, delighted to play along, did the same. He winked at Mandi and both Nathan and Jaci slipped into the elevator.

"Did you enjoy yourself?" Nathan asked dryly once they were safely ensconced in the elevator. "I thought you played it a little over-the-top, don't you?"

"What about you, you giant flirt? And for the record, that girl is a ditz. There's no way she ought to be manning the front desk at a place like this. It's a wonder you haven't been hacked before."

"I think she's the daughter of someone important. She showed up and replaced the stern-looking man who'd been at the front desk since I started."

"Nepotism strikes again," Jaci muttered. "I hate when people get a leg up just because of who they're related to. I lost out on a huge advertising client because suddenly his son, who had just graduated from college, wanted to try his hand at 'making ads and stuff,' as junior had put it. That job was going to pay my rent for a year." She sighed, trying not to be bitter about old history, but she was nervous and eager to think about anything aside from the task at hand. "Well, my one consolation was that the ad campaign tanked and they lost millions of dollars on junior's ridiculous idea. I know that's not nice of me but... Sorry...I'm rambling."

"Are you okay?" he asked her, eyeing her curiously.

"Yes, why?" She stiffened, hating that she was so damn transparent. Maybe that's why she never became a spy—that and the fact that she valued human life. She made a conscious effort to relax and tried her smile again.

He nodded in approval and said, "Okay, when we get inside, let me do the talking. It's important that Tom not sense that anything is amiss."

"Right. Just smile and nod like a good little puppet."

"Something like that. Are you capable of simply smiling and nodding like a good puppet?" he teased and she rolled her eyes at his question.

"Only when properly motivated," she replied dryly, rubbing her hands on her dress before she was introduced to the man who was trying to kill *her* man. Sweaty, clammy palms were simply not a great way to start a relationship; not to mention it might tip Tom off that they were onto him.

The doors slid open with a metal groan and Nathan led her down the corridor to a closed double door. He knocked twice and then walked in, seemingly just as he always did and Jaci followed with her dopey smile plastered on her face and hopefully love-struck stars in her eyes. *Oh, please let this work!*

* * *

Tom jumped when Nathan walked in and after recognizing who had interrupted him, a tremulous smile followed. "There you are! Where have you been, my boy? Cryptic emails are enough to send an old man into a heart attack," he teased, his gaze alighting on Jaci quizzically. "And who is your lovely lady friend?"

"Sorry I've been incommunicado for the past few days but I needed to spend some quality time with my girl, Jaci Williams."

Something flickered in Tom's eyes and Nathan wasn't sure if it was confusion or guilt but it was definitely not something good. So far, Tom was exhibiting every classic sign of subterfuge from the darting gaze to the slight tremble in his fingers as he clenched them together in a seemingly innocent gesture. "Your girl? I didn't realize you were dating again."

"She took pity on me and took me back," Nathan answered, linking his fingers through hers for emphasis. "Hey, the reason I've stopped by is because I need to cash in some of my vacation time. We have plans to do some traveling."

"Yes, yes, I'm sure you have plenty on the books," Tom said, the lines on his face seeming deeper. He swallowed and glanced out the window to the city below. "Good to see you, Nathan. I was worried."

"Worried? Why?" Nathan asked, forcing a casualness to his tone that he didn't feel. His nerves were strung tighter than bowstrings as he held his breath waiting for Tom to tip his hand somehow.

Tom seemed to hear what he'd just said and backtracked clumsily, saying, "Nothing, nothing. So travel, eh? Sounds good," he said, as he rubbed his forehead with his forefingers. "I'm sorry, I haven't been feeling well. I can't seem to shake this miserable cold."

"You poor thing," Jaci murmured and glanced at Nathan purposefully. "We should let him get back to work so he can finish and go home and rest."

"Yeah," he agreed, adding with a slightly narrowed stare. "One last thing before we go.... I was thinking of taking your advice and investing. What was that company you were talking about a few months back? Tessara something or another?"

At the mention of his company, Tom looked up and his stare sharpened. "Why the sudden interest?"

Nathan's stomach clenched at the raw emotion in Tom's eyes and affected a casual shrug. "I just figured you've never steered me wrong before and I needed to broaden my investment portfolio. I trust your judgment." He let that sentiment sit between them and he hoped Tom felt the crush of his conscience before he continued, "Besides, maybe I'll do as well as you and I can buy my own pleasure cruiser."

"Well, yes, yes, investing is good. But give it a little time. You don't want to jump into anything prematurely." He slid paperwork across the desk for Nathan to sign and Nathan saw it was a request for time off. Nathan signed his name and acted as if it was just another day when in fact, he wanted to yell at the man for betraying him.

Why, Tom? Nathan almost wanted Tom to simply admit that he'd been the one to put the hit out on him because it would beat this terrible hole growing in Nathan's heart. Tom shook a few pills into his hand and tossed them back with a swallow of water and Nathan couldn't help but wonder if a guilty conscience was eating at him or if it was something else. Nathan paused at the door and Tom looked as if poised to say something but he thought better of it and simply waved him on with a brittle smile.

"Could he act more guilty?" Jaci whispered as they walked to the elevator. "Do you need any more proof that your boss sold you out?"

He remained silent. He didn't want to talk about it. Yeah, Tom looked guilty, all right, but there was something else lurking behind the guilt that kept snagging Nathan's train of thought. *Fear.*

Tom had been afraid of something and Nathan didn't think it was him. Maybe he was still trying to find a reason—any reason to believe in Tom—but he knew he had to talk to Tom away from the office. And without Jaci.

Chapter 19

Nathan hadn't spoken much since leaving his office and Jaci didn't know how to broach the subject that was likely weighing on his mind. But as she opened her mouth to say something—anything—Nathan cut in with his plan.

"I will take you back to the safe house—"

"No way," she interrupted, putting her foot down. There was no way she was going to stay in that house. "We can stay at my place. Obviously they wouldn't assume that we would go there, because it's the last place we should go."

"That's some dizzying logic and I'm not willing to bank our lives on it," Nathan said. "But if you're not willing to stay at the safe house then we will have to stay at a motel. We can pay with cash so our credit cards aren't traced. But I doubt a motel will be any better than the safe house accommodations."

"Why? Even a creepy little motel has clean sheets and running water," she countered. "So what happens next? Can you go to the authorities? Maybe the FBI or the CIA or some other branch of the government that's not so clandestine? Maybe they'd like to know that someone within ID is running amok? That's got to be worth something, right?"

Nathan grunted in response and she wasn't quite sure if he agreed or disagreed. He'd officially gone into silent mode, which wasn't helpful at all. "Care to share? Inquiring minds want to know."

He sighed and focused on the road. "Tom was like a father to me. My own father was an ass and out of my life so early. It's hard to reconcile that Tom wasn't who he pretended to be."

Jaci could appreciate that; that's pretty much how she'd felt when Nathan had dumped her so unceremoniously. She reached over and caressed his shoulder. "I'm sorry. That really sucks."

He accepted her commiseration but otherwise remained silent and she exhaled a long breath, wishing he would share his feelings. But that was Nathan in a nutshell—stoic. "We'll swing by McDonald's and pick up some grub and then check into the hotel," he said, changing lanes to switch to a different freeway. "Then after we're settled in the hotel, and I'm sure that no one has followed us, I have some other errands to run while you stay behind."

"Like hell I am. Do we have to go over this again? It's not a hard concept to grasp. I'm not leaving your side. Besides, don't you watch movies? The girl who gets left behind is the one who gets murdered."

"You'll be fine. But if it would make you feel more secure, I'll leave you with my gun."

"I guess I'd feel more secure if I knew *how* to shoot a gun. With my luck I'd end up shooting off my foot."

"I won't be gone long. But there are some things I can't do with you on my tail. Will you trust me?"

Jaci bit her lip, knowing that he was asking her to take a leap of faith, but she was a little short in the trust department—especially when it came to him being honest with her. "Promise me you're not going to go off on your own and go back to Tom's," she said.

"I'm not going to do anything that will put me in harm's way," he said, neatly sidestepping her request. But she wasn't dumb and because he actually thought she'd fall for something so transparent, she reached over and pinched him for trying to evade her question.

He yelped and cast her a dirty look. "What was that for? Are you trying to make us crash?" he asked, irritated.

"You treat me like I'm stupid. Just tell me the truth. Are you going to Tom or not? I know something's been bothering you since we left the building and because you won't tell me I can only assume that it's something you think I don't want to hear. So just level with me.... Are you going back to Tom?"

"Relax," Nathan said. "I have to run by my place

and pick up some more ammo and guns—it's not like I can walk into the gun shop and buy new supplies. But I have an arsenal in my house as well as extra cash that we're going to need, so chill out and just relax in the hotel, okay? Maybe enjoy a bath and decompress a little. You've been through a lot in a short period of time. You need to unplug for a bit for your sanity. Trust me, I know how it feels to burn both ends of the candle and the result is pretty ugly."

Was she being a total toad because she didn't believe him? She couldn't escape the niggling sense that he was telling her what she wanted to hear so she wouldn't worry. She hated that she just couldn't take him at his word. But if anything happened to him, she'd die—possibly literally.

"I don't want you to get hurt."

Nathan heard the sincerity in her voice and he backed down, actually smiling at her. "I'll be fine. I feel naked without supplies and have everything I need back at my place. But I can't take you with me because on the off chance that someone is watching my house, I don't want them to see or target you."

She relented. His explanation made a bit of sense. And then she felt like a butt for not believing him. "Okay," she agreed. "But don't take too long because my imagination will go crazy and I might have to go looking for you."

"Do not come looking for me. I promise I won't take too long. But I need to know that you are safe so please, stay put."

She smiled. "Well, when you put it so nicely..." Then she tapped her cheek for a kiss. He chuckled and leaned in but as he went to press a kiss to her cheek, she turned and he caught her lips instead. He swept his tongue through her mouth and she smiled against his lips.

He pulled away, knowing in his eyes. "You did that on purpose," he accused lightly and she didn't deny it.

She wanted all of this to be over so they could spend more time kissing and less time running for their lives. Jaci sighed and wondered if that day was ever going to happen.

Nathan waited in the shadows of Tom's stately house to ensure he was alone before he let himself in through the back patio. Nathan flipped the latch silently and remembered a conversation he'd had with Tom once about the lax security on his own home.

"You, of all people, know how important a good security system is," Nathan had scolded Tom when he'd seen the flimsy lock mechanism on the back patio door. "This is your worst vulnerability. Do you know how easily I could gain access to your home with this lock? You might as well leave it unlocked with a Welcome Intruder sign on the door."

But Tom had laughed off Nathan's warning, saying, "You worry too much. You're going to turn gray prematurely. Besides, I have two dogs who would chew off an intruder's face before they could get very far."

It was true that Zeus and Magnus, two Dobermans,

were fierce enough in looks, but in actuality they were big lovers who would rather lick a person to death than chew someone's face off as Tom had boasted. Case in point, the two dogs had trotted over to Nathan the minute he'd breached the backyard and whined for pats on the head and bacon treats.

Nathan listened to the sounds of the house and heard the faint strain of a television coming from the den. He stealthily made his way toward the sound and when he saw Tom's silhouette reclining in his large overstuffed chair, he walked into the room, startling Tom so badly, his face immediately paled. "N-Nathan? What are you doing here?" he asked, his gaze darting.

"It's time to cut the bullshit, Tom," Nathan said, his mouth firming against the distasteful business at hand. "Why'd you do it?"

Tom's lip trembled and for the first time Nathan saw the press of time weighing on the older man. He appeared to have aged overnight as deep lines carved grooves into his skin and more white had populated itself through his thinning hair. "I don't know what you're talking about..."

"You were like a father to me," Nathan said, cutting into the excuses and the lies. "I trusted you."

Tom shook his head, mopping his suddenly damp forehead with his hand, seemingly frustrated by the turn of events. "Nathan, you have to go. I will talk to you later but not now. There's more at stake than you know and I don't have the time to explain. Take your girl and go find a place to hole up for a few weeks."

Nathan frowned, thrown off guard. "What's going on? Did you order the hit on me?" Tom looked wounded and ashamed at the same time and Nathan didn't know what to think. If anything he was more confused than ever but he desperately wanted to believe that Tom hadn't been involved, no matter how incriminating the circumstantial evidence appeared. A different thought occurred to Nathan as he peered at his mentor. "Are you in some kind of trouble?"

"I never wanted you to get hurt but you kept asking questions. I told you to drop it but you wouldn't let it go," Tom said, rising from his chair to go to the bar, where he poured himself a shaky drink. "Things got out of hand so quickly..."

"What got out of hand?" Nathan asked. "Tom, you're not making any sense."

Tom turned and his mouth trembled as if he were crumbling from the inside out and he simply shook his head and finished his whiskey in one swallow. "You have to believe that I never wanted you to get mixed up in any of this. I don't even know how it all happened and why it turned bad. It seemed a simple thing—make a little extra money with a good investment—but nothing is ever simple. I should've known."

Nathan was losing his patience. "Tom, if you don't start making some sense I'm going to have to report your actions to your superior." But Nathan's threat bounced off Tom as if he hadn't even heard. Tom seemed locked in his own world, mumbling to himself and pouring shot after shot, numbing something inside only he knew about. Frustrated, Nathan grabbed Tom by the lapels of his shirt and jerked him around to face him. "Did you know about the hit on me and Jaci?" he ground out, his teeth clenched.

"Only after the fact," Tom whispered but his eyes welled. "I had no choice. She was going to ruin me if I didn't keep quiet and I took the coward's way out. By the time I realized what was happening, I was in too deep to pull out. I'm sorry."

"Who?" Nathan asked, searching his mentor's face. "Who are you so afraid of?"

Tom opened his mouth to answer but there was a small popping sound as a projectile punctured the glass window, burying itself in Tom's skull, effectively ending the conversation. Tom's eyes rolled back in his head and he collapsed into Nathan's arms. *NO!* Nathan helped Tom's body to the ground and came away with his hands red from the small wound as it began to weep a river of blood. *Damn it!*

"What have you gotten yourself into, Tom?" he muttered as he stepped away, careful to stay clear of the spreading blood pool. He surveyed the shatter pattern on the glass to try and gauge the distance the shot was taken from and took careful note of the surrounding vantage points based on the trajectory of the bullet. He knew from the concentric fracture of the glass, which was relatively clean and unblemished, the shot had come from long range—a sniper hit. He ducked away from the window, knowing whoever had fired the shot might still be watching, putting Nathan in the crosshairs, too.

His DNA was everywhere and there was no time to clean up. Using his forearms he flipped on the water faucet at the kitchen sink and rinsed his hands, then raced into the laundry room and grabbed the bleach with a paper towel to prevent fingerprints. He poured the bleach down the drain to destroy the blood evidence and then sprinted out the patio door to melt into the night.

Chapter 20

Jaci had just finished a bath in the reasonably clean bathtub at the hotel when Nathan hurried through the door and quickly rebolted the lock. She could tell he was rattled but when he turned and she saw blood splatter on his jeans, she thought the worst. "You've been shot again?" she cried, rushing to him but he barked at her to keep away as he stripped. "What do you mean 'keep away'?" she asked, confused and hurt.

"It's not my blood," he explained in a curt tone as he made quick work of stripping naked. He strode nude into the bathroom and turned the water on full blast, then while the water heated back up, he scooped the bloody clothes and stuffed them into the dry cleaning bag and tied it tightly closed. He said to her, "I have a change of clothes in the backseat of the truck. Go get them and bring them to me while I scrub down." At her reluctance, he gave her a hard look and pointed, "Go! I'll explain in a minute but I need to get clean."

Jaci jerked a small nod and quickly unbolted the lock with shaking fingers and ran to the truck to find what he'd asked for. A small bag was tucked beneath the driver side seat and she pulled it free. She ran back to the hotel and slammed the door, her heart hammering and her mind going to the worst of places. Nathan emerged from the steamy bathroom, toweling off, and she tossed him the clothes. "Did you kill someone?" she asked, almost afraid to know the answer.

"No," he bit out. "But someone is most definitely dead and it's going to look like I did it if we don't get some answers real quick. They couldn't frame me for your death because you're still alive so they found someone else to kill and blame me for."

"Who?"

"Tom."

She gasped. "Tom? Where did you see Tom?" At his stubborn set of his jaw she knew he'd gone to Tom in spite of promising that he wouldn't. "I knew you were lying to me," she said with a hurt tone. "Why?"

"Focus, Jaci! Tom is dead and he was killed in his own house. He was just about to tell me who was in on this scheme and then *bam!* A bullet went slamming through his brain, ending his confession."

"He was confessing? To what? Trying to kill you?"

"Not exactly. Honestly, it was a bit jumbled what he

was saying, but from what I understood, someone else was pulling the strings and Tom was forced to dance to their tune."

"So you think Tom was innocent?"

"No. I think he was guilty of allowing some bad things to happen but I know he didn't mean for situations to go that far. Tom was a good man who made some bad judgments. That makes far more sense than the idea that Tom was a rotten apple."

Jaci shook her head, unable to process everything at once. She sat on the edge of the bed while Nathan finished dressing. "So…what are you saying? Tom wasn't the bad guy?" she asked plaintively and Nathan cast her a sharp, disapproving glance.

"Well, now we're back to square one," she said, frustrated. "Where are we supposed to start if Tom wasn't the one calling the shots?" Her eyes welled up and she couldn't help herself. "What are we supposed to do now?"

"Jase, don't fall apart on me now." He gripped her by the shoulders and peered into her eyes with a hard stare. "I need you sharp. I know this is a lot to take in but I think I have an idea of who shot Tom."

She stared. "You do? How?"

"Tom was hit by a sniper and at pretty long range. My guess is that someone from ID, someone with plenty of long-range sniper experience, made the hit. Which means there's more than one bad egg running around the department."

"I don't see how that helps. How many people do

you have working for ID? There have to be hundreds. What are you going to do, question every single employee to find who might've done this?"

"I don't need to question every employee. There's only one I need to question."

"Who?"

"Miko." Jaci's mouth gaped open. He nodded at her shock, still reeling from the gut hunch himself. "There were two people working at ID who excelled in long-range hits. Me and Miko. When Miko went out on a medical that left only me. When we saw him the other day there was something about his behavior that threw me off. His microexpressions kept telling a different story than what his mouth was saying. I didn't want to believe it—I was too focused on the possibility that Tom was the one ordering the hit that I ignored my gut instinct."

"I don't understand. Miko is your friend. Why would he want to hurt you?"

"He didn't hurt me. He hurt Tom. I suspect he hadn't expected that I would be there with Tom tonight but even so the bullet is still lodged in Tom's brain. Someone less experienced might've picked the wrong caliber bullet and I might've gotten hit as well. I'm almost positive it was Miko. The question is why."

"Do you think Miko lied about the medical discharge?" she asked. "Do you think he's been working on the side under the radar for someone within ID?"

"I don't know. But I know he was paranoid about something. The only way to find out is to ask him."

"Are you crazy?" she exclaimed, unable to believe he would make such a foolish suggestion. "What is with you wanting to go and talk to the people who you think are trying to kill you? One of these days those people are going to succeed. I say we go to Mexico. I have my passport—we can be out of here and sitting on a sunny beach by tomorrow morning."

"I'm not leaving until I know what happened. No one is forcing me from the life I worked hard to build. I'm not running."

Frustration and fear caused her voice to rise as she stomped her foot for being unable to get through to him. "Don't you want a life together?" she asked. "Don't you think that all this macho crap is unrealistic in the long term? Sometimes the bad guys get away. That's life. I'd rather continue breathing and be called a coward than be dead and be on the right side of an argument."

"I know you can't possibly understand. And I'm not asking you to. I'm not even asking you to stay and wait for me. All I'm saying is that I can't run. I'm going to find out who's behind all this corruption and take them down. One way or another."

Jaci's eyes welled again and she wanted to throw something at him. *Stubborn man!* "Do my feelings count at all in this?"

Nathan's jaw hardened and he looked away. "I've made my decision. I'm sorry it doesn't gel with what you think is right. But the bottom line is that I'm willing to pay the ultimate price for doing what is right. We don't know how far this corruption goes. How many more innocent lives might go down because I did not take the risk? I can't live with that. And if you knew what I lived with under a normal basis you wouldn't ask me to."

Shame crept up Jaci's neck and she swallowed when she felt it was choking her. He was right. She was being selfish. If more innocent people died, she'd never be able to forgive herself. "I love you, Nathan," she said miserably. "I don't want to lose you and it seems at every turn there's the certainty of death or breaking up!"

His expression softened and he caressed her cheek. "I'll do my best to come back to you. But if I don't, don't wait. Take your passport and go. Find those sunny beaches in Mexico and live the way that you were meant to. It's my fault that your life has been compromised and I never wanted this for you. Protecting you has been my primary mission and if I fail at that, I might as well take a bullet to the head because life wouldn't be worth living."

"Don't you say your goodbyes. Not yet." Jaci wiped her eyes, her gaze narrowing as she pulled herself together by the thinnest margins. "Fine. You're off to go chase the bad guys, then I'm going to chase them with you. I'd rather die *with* you than live a lifetime alone *without* you."

"Jaci, you don't know what you're saying..."

"Like hell I don't. I know what I want in life and if you're telling me this is what you need to do in order to start a new life with me, then let's get it over with. Hopefully, when it's all over, we both end up on the other side—*alive.*"

Nathan couldn't believe the strength of this woman. He cupped her face and drew her in for a kiss. "I hate the idea of you in harm's way. Don't you get that I would do anything to protect you?"

She held his stare as a slow smile crept across her face. "Then you'd better teach me how to shoot a gun. I want to be armed and dangerous, too."

"You little vixen, that's the hottest thing I've ever heard you say," he said, capturing her mouth again in a hard kiss. Their tongues tangled in a brutal and almost violent dance and when they broke apart, they were both breathing heavily. Her eyes glittered with desire and he could barely contain his urge to simply throw her down and yank her clothes off. But her idea was solid. She needed to know how to protect herself and he was the best person to teach her. "I think that's a great idea," he said, pulling her to her feet.

He settled in behind her, swallowing a groan when her pert rear end pressed into his groin, momentarily distracting him from his true purpose. Using his .45 caliber semiautomatic Glock for demonstration, he quickly emptied the chamber and removed the magazine, then he showed her how to disengage the safety and how to properly place her hands. "Keep your finger outside the trigger guard," he instructed her softly.

"We don't want any accidents. Don't put your finger on the trigger until you're ready to shoot."

"Like this?" she asked, cocking her head to the side as she concentrated. He caught a whiff of her unique scent and he closed his eyes against the assault on his senses. "It's heavier than I imagined it would be," she admitted. "Does your arm ever get tired lugging this thing around?"

"I didn't even notice the weight. I've carried much heavier." Talking guns and having a beautiful woman pressed up against him were wreaking havoc on his resolve. Even as he tried to remain focused, his penis hadn't received the memo that it wasn't playtime. Within seconds an erection had begun to grow behind his zipper. He cleared his throat and tried to focus. "The magazine goes in like this," he slapped the magazine into the end of the gun. "Now wrap your other hand around the other side of the frame, so that you align your two thumbs to point downrange. Pay attention, this is important. Make sure both thumbs clear the slide or hammer. You don't want to get hurt firing your own gun."

She glanced up at him. "Has that ever happened to you?" she asked.

"No," he said. "But I saw it happen to a guy in basic training. It was funnier than hell."

"Probably wasn't funny to him."

He shrugged. "Probably not. I think it broke his thumb. One thing's for sure, he never did that again." He positioned his hands on her hips. "Now widen your stance a little and don't lock your legs. You want to have a little bit of bend to your legs, otherwise you could pass out. Balance is very important. Now, with a firm grip on the gun, go ahead and take aim. You want to line the front sight with the rear sight using your dominant eye and closing the other one. You got that?"

She nodded.

"You want to aim for center mass. You should see the sharply focused front sight as your main focus. Now when you go to fire, if you can, time it with that of your breath. Take a breath, let out half and then squeeze the trigger." She followed his instruction and fired an empty round.

She turned to him and smiled. "That wasn't so bad. It was actually kind of fun."

He grinned. "Well, let's see how you do with actual bullets in the gun. Also, most people aren't prepared for the sound of the shot and it startles them. For first timers, it can be a little jarring. My hope is that you won't have to use it but I feel a little better knowing that I've at least shown you the basics."

"I hope I never am forced to shoot a person but I will if I have to."

He nodded in approval. "That's my girl. Don't hesitate because they won't hesitate to kill you. Do you understand?"

She nodded gravely. He tipped her head back and sealed his mouth to hers and removed the gun from her fingers. "That concludes the lesson on how to defend yourself against the bad guys," he said as she turned in his arms. He tossed the gun onto the bed and then filled his palms with a generous squeeze of her luscious behind. She hopped into his arms and he groaned when she rubbed her hot core against his midsection. "Woman, you are so perfect. Packing heat with a body that could stop a man's heart.... How did I get so damn lucky?"

"Less talk, more action," she demanded in an impatient breathy tone, slanting her mouth over his as she pulled his shirt free from his body. "That's an order, soldier."

"Roger that," he grinned as they tumbled to the bed. Tonight he was going to forget about tomorrow and simply love this incredible woman. And judging by the way she was moaning with pleasure, she was totally on board with that idea.

Tomorrow would come soon enough—and with it, only God knew what.

Chapter 21

Nathan spent the morning surveilling Miko and in the late afternoon followed him to the bar. Both Nathan and Jaci slipped through the back door and quickly went up the stairs. For some reason Miko's hired thug wasn't on duty. That in itself, Nathan found odd. Given how paranoid Miko had been the last time they'd spoken, Nathan found the absence of the guard troubling.

"Going somewhere?" Nathan asked when he saw Miko shoving papers into a briefcase. That explained no guard. Miko wasn't planning to stick around. "So how much of that horse shit that you told me was actually true?"

Miko startled when he saw Nathan and Jaci, his bloodshot eyes not those of a healthy man and Nathan felt a pang for his old friend. "I wanted out," Miko said. "That part was true."

"What's going on?" Nathan peered at his friend, needing the truth. "Come on, man, we didn't go through so much to end like this."

Miko shook his head, as if overwhelmed by impossible choices and continued to shove papers into his briefcase. "It started off so easy to justify. And the money was good—too good. But what can I say? There are no good excuses for what I've done. And now it's all fallen to shit. I should've known I was taking a devil's bargain."

"Why, Miko?" Nathan didn't bother pretending. Miko knew why Nathan was there. "What the hell are you mixed up with?"

Miko barked a short laugh, the sound desperate as he fell into his chair and regarded Nathan with something akin to fatal respect. "You were smart. You started asking questions. I didn't. And when a job came my way that sounded wrong, the deal was sweetened with more money. And I took it. You're not that kind of person. And they know it and that's why you had to go. It was supposed to be a murder-suicide. Clean, no questions asked. They were going to falsify your military records, insert some instabilities so no one would question when you snapped and killed your girlfriend and shot yourself. It was messed up and there wasn't a damn thing I could do about it. Because by that point I was already in too deep."

"Who ordered the hit on Tom?" Nathan asked. "I thought Tom was in charge but I was wrong, wasn't I?"

"She's everywhere. She's got eyes in the sky—she's got ears on the street. There is no escaping her reach. And if she wants you dead, it's gonna happen. Tom, the poor old bastard, became a liability. The minute he tried to stop what she wanted with you, he got put on the list."

Nathan took a step forward. "Who the hell are you talking about? What list?" he demanded to know. "Who is this woman?" Tom had mentioned a woman, as well. "Are there more people on her hit list?"

"She's the freaking devil," Miko answered with a defeated smile. "And when she owns your soul, there is no getting out. But I'm tired. I'm so tired, Nathan. I used to be a good guy. I was one of the good guys," he said with a sudden show of passion. "I saved lives, damn it. We both did. When did it all change?"

Nathan shared a look with Jaci, frustrated. "I can't help you if I don't know who I'm fighting. Tell me, and I'll bring the bitch down."

"She probably has my office bugged. She doesn't trust anyone, not even the people who hide her dirty secrets." Miko's gaze roamed his office. "I always wanted to own a bar. I thought there was something nostalgic and cool about being a pub owner. But just like anything, it's all an illusion. It sucks as much as anything else. There's nothing golden anymore."

"So what are you going to do, bug out? Run like a coward?" Nathan asked, angry. "You can help fix this.

You could make it right. You have a chance to be the good guy again."

At that, Miko chuckled. "I love you, man. But you don't know what you're talking about. There's no going back from what I've done. I have blood on my hands."

"We *all* have blood on our hands. That's just the way it is. We were soldiers. We did the work no one else wanted. And when we took the job with ID, when we thought we were doing the right thing—once again we did the jobs that no one else could do. Don't turn this around. Not every assignment was rigged. I know that in my heart."

Miko squeezed his eyes shut and tears leaked around the closed lids. "I'm sorry, man. I never wanted it to end like this. I liked playing the hero. It felt good. Tromping around the desert of Iraq, facing down insurgents and dodging IEDs felt a hell of a lot better than this moment right now. That time spent in hell was just practice for what's going down right now."

"Give me a name."

Miko reached into his drawer and withdrew his gun. Nathan stilled, his hand going to his own weapon. "What are you doing?" he asked, a sliver of dread curling around his spine. "Don't," he warned.

"If anyone can stop her...maybe it's you," Miko said softly. He caught Nathan's gaze and held it a heartbeat. "Look more deeply into Tessara Pharm," he said, before tipping his head back and blowing a hole through his chin.

* * *

Jaci screamed as everything happened in slow motion. Nathan sprang for the gun a second too late before the bullet ripped through Miko's flesh, splattering brain matter against the wall. She turned away before she threw up, drawing in deep gasping breaths as shock began to eat away at her ability to remain upright. Before she knew it, Nathan's grip bit into her arm as he dragged her away from the scene and down the stairs as they fled to the truck.

"What happened? I don't understand why he would do that," Jaci moaned, her teeth beginning to chatter. "I…I…didn't see it coming," she said, grinding her eyes to wipe away the image stuck there. She would never sleep again as long as that memory remained fresh. Tears began to fall as a reflex and she couldn't stop even though she tried. Soon enough her shoulders were racked by deep, ugly sobs that seemed to come from her stomach. She braced herself on the dash as she tried to get ahold of herself but she was quickly losing her grip. "I don't want to see anyone else die!"

"Jaci! Listen to me. You're going into shock. Take a deep breath and focus on calming your breathing. You can do this." He navigated the city streets with one eye on the road and one on her and the fact that she was disintegrating without being able to stop the deterioration scared her even worse. The air squeezed from her lungs as she fought to breathe and black dots danced before her eyes. "I-I-I c-c-can't breathe!" she managed to gasp and she vaguely heard Nathan curse as he wrenched the wheel to detour down a side street and then duck into an alley. He slammed the brakes and caught her just as she lost consciousness.

Jaci drifted in a black cloud of nothingness and relief followed by the realization that she no longer felt fear or worry or anything. All the events of the past week had disappeared like mist in the warm sunshine and she was happy to float in oblivion for a while longer. If she were dying, wasn't her life supposed to flash before her eyes? She saw nothing. Surely her life had contained enough to create a highlight reel, right?

Or maybe she wasn't dying but simply refusing to return to consciousness. Yeah, that was probably it. Too many people dying. *Right in front of her.* She couldn't handle it. And to think, her biggest worry at one time was whether she'd eaten too many carbs at lunch. Who was that girl? She didn't know any longer. That girl seemed light years away from who she was now.

Jaci turned and closed her eyes against the faint sound of someone calling her name. No. Her lids popped back open. She didn't want to go back. But the caller became more insistent and the black, comforting fog began to lift. *Nooo!* Jaci startled as something sucked at her feet, drawing her out of her sweet oblivion and popping her back into the here and now. She opened her eyes and this time, Nathan's face came into view, his expression panicked as he lightly tapped her face in an annoying fashion. She swatted at his hand as she came to and he helped her to sit up. "I fainted, didn't I?" she asked.

"You hyperventilated and passed out. That's why I was telling you to breathe."

"All I was doing was breathing and that seemed to cause the problem," she retorted, irritated. She squinted at the sudden pain throbbing behind her temple. "Ouch. My head hurts," she complained, shooting him a dark look. "How hard did you tap my face?"

"Not hard enough to give you a headache," he answered with a scowl. "When you hyperventilate it causes a loss of carbon dioxide from your body, which causes the headache." He waited a minute then asked, "Are you okay?"

"No," she admitted with a shake of her head. "I want to be okay but every time I think I can handle this, someone else dies right in front of me and unlike you, that's not a regular part of my day. I freak out when I hit a squirrel on the road. I'm not cut out for all this crazy stuff," she confessed with a sad sniff, hating that she wasn't the Rambo girl she wanted to be for him. "I'm sorry." The silence in the truck made her sorry for saying anything. Did he regret meeting her? Had she totally disappointed him? She wouldn't be surprised; she'd disappointed herself. She sniffed. "They make it look a lot easier in the movies," she observed, risking a tiny glance at him.

"Yeah," he agreed, pulling away to stare out the window at the passing cars on the street. "I can't promise things won't get worse. Hell, I can't even guarantee your safety at this point, Jase. The only way I can figure to keep you out of danger is to send you away. I have plenty of cash and you have your passport. Your idea of Mexico is sounding pretty good right now."

"You mean, you and I splitting for Mexico," she asked in a small voice. "Or…just me?"

He wouldn't look at her and she had her answer.

But this time…she didn't argue.

Nathan knew this was the right decision but as he shoved wads of cash into a duffel for Jaci, he felt sick to his stomach. Maybe it was because he knew this was probably the last time he'd see her. Chances were he wouldn't make it out of this mission alive. Whoever he was up against had considerable power and she had a distinct advantage in that he didn't have a clue who she was. All he knew was that it was a woman calling the shots—and an evil one at that.

He wanted Jaci far away from anyone like that.

"Don't stop until you reach the border. I don't care what you hear, okay? Just get in the car and keep driving. A moving target is far less vulnerable," he instructed her sternly, focusing on the task of putting her in a safe place. "Once you cross the border, there's a hotel in San Felipe called the Casa en el Mar. Ask for Alejandro and tell him I sent you. He will take care of you until I can join you."

She lifted her gaze to him and in her eyes he saw the question she was afraid to ask. What if he didn't make it back to her? His throat closed. He couldn't lie to her and offer false assurances even if it would make her feel better in the short term. "Trust no one but Alejandro. You should have enough cash to last you for at least six months. Don't come back any sooner. Do you hear me?" Tears sparkled in her eyes and she nodded. He ought to put her in the car and hope for the best. But when she found her way into his arms, he held on for dear life. He kissed her crown, inhaling the scent of coconut and cucumbers from her favorite shampoo and wished he could bottle up her scent to take with him. He pressed a quick kiss to her forehead and then reluctantly put her into the cheap car he'd bought with cash. "Remember..."

"Trust no one," she murmured with a nod of understanding. She caught his hand and kissed it before he could push away from the car. "Be safe and get this finished." Her eyes glittered with unshed tears as she said with a brave smile, "I'll be waiting for you. I'll be the girl in the green-striped bikini."

I love you. I love you. I love you. He nodded, unable to get the words past his lips as he watched her pull away.

He turned his back on her retreating car and switched modes.

Time to hunt down an out-of-control bitch and put her down.

For good.

Chapter 22

Nathan needed help finding more about Tessara and he knew just the person to do that but as he bounded the stairs to James and Jaci's apartment, he found the door kicked open and the interior destroyed. He did a quick perimeter search and finding nothing, split the scene. He dialed the burner phone and hoped James had had the good sense to grab it before he hightailed it out of the apartment. The phone rang four times but just as it was about to switch to voice mail, James came on the line, agitated and freaking out. "Is that you, Jase?" he asked.

"No, it's Nathan. What happened to your place?" he asked, getting straight to the point. "Are you hurt?"

"I'm fine but I sensed someone was tailing me and so I packed up my laptop and a few essentials to hide out for a while until things chilled out. I thought maybe I was overreacting but then I went back to my place to get a few things and saw that someone had totally trashed it!"

"You've got one helluva guardian angel on your side," Nathan murmured. "Okay, we have to meet. Things have gotten hot and I need your help finding information on the company Tessara Pharmaceutical. Got that?"

"Yeah, Tessara Pharm. That ought to be easy," James said. "Haven't you been watching the news?"

"I've been a little busy," Nathan bit out, irritated. "So what's the deal with this company?"

"They've had some kind of medical breakthrough for cancer research. The company is worth billions."

"Billions?" Nathan repeated, thinking of Tom and how he'd been living the high life for a while. "Has there been anything on the news about a man named Tom Wyatt? Remember? He was part owner of Tessara."

"Yeah, tough break for him. Heart attack right before this big announcement."

"It was no heart attack," he muttered. "He was shot and killed but I'm guessing the story released to the press is a bit more whitewashed."

"Papers said that Wyatt was found in his home by his housekeeper, dead of a heart attack in his bed."

More smoke and mirrors. "I need you to find out more about the remaining owners of Tessara. The last words a source uttered to me before he blew his brains out were to dig more deeply into Tessara. The answers are there somewhere. In the meantime, I'm going to tap a resource I have within the Department of Defense. I think it's time to bring in some additional firepower."

"It must be nice to have friends in high places," James said. "I have a friend who works at Microsoft but he can't even get me free programming."

"I wouldn't call this person a friend…but he might be willing to make a few inquiries. I helped him get into the officer training program a few years ago. We'll see how far that gets me."

"How's Jase holding up?" James ventured and Nathan felt himself bristle before he could stop it. He had to stop being so possessive about her. Before he could answer, James said, "I didn't like that you were back in the picture but, man, I'm glad she's with you. When I saw my apartment trashed, all I could think of was how glad I was that Jaci wasn't anywhere near when it happened. No telling what the thugs might've done to her."

He grunted in agreement, not sure how to accept James's gratitude when he'd been seconds away from biting the man's head off for even asking about Jaci. He rubbed at his forehead. "Yeah. Me, too," he said, switching subjects abruptly. "Call me as soon as you find something and do yourself a favor and stay out of open spaces."

He heard James audibly gulp as he said, "Thanks for the tip, man."

"Don't mention it," Nathan muttered and ended the call.

Nathan dialed a number that he had never expected to call and he sure as hell could bet the man on the other end wasn't going to throw a party when he realized who was calling.

"Hey, Jake…I need your help."

Nathan hadn't exactly been honest with Jaci about his brother's whereabouts but with a little brother who worked for the Department of Defense in a highly classified branch of the government, he felt it was better to simply make up a story rather than go with the truth. Besides, it wasn't as if they were chummy and went out golfing together on Sundays. Fact of the matter was, Jake probably preferred to forget he had a brother at all.

Jake, a tall man built similarly to Nathan, exited his car and scanned the underground parking garage, his eyes sharp and wary. Nathan felt a pang of pride that he had no right to feel at seeing how well Jakey had turned out.

Nathan emerged from the shadow of the cement pillar and Jake's expression didn't change. His brother had grown up. Gone was the chubby-cheeked boy who had followed him around, pestering him incessantly until Nathan wanted to punt him off a bridge. Now not a hint of that baby fat remained on his carved angular cheekbones. Hell, his brother was almost pretty. If situations had been way different—as in different childhoods and born to different parents—maybe they might've ribbed each other but as it was, they were strangers. The only reason Jake had even shown up was because he didn't like owing anyone anything—not even his brother—and he wanted to cash in that chip and be done with it. "I don't recall you being melodramatic so I assume you're in a heap of trouble to have put so much effort into not being seen," Jake said. "What's going on?"

"You look good," Nathan said and Jake's expression flickered but he didn't return the sentiment. Nathan read between the lines clearly. "Listen, I wouldn't involve you if I didn't think I needed you but there's something rotten going on in ID and I know you're about the only person I can trust with the information."

At the mention of ID, Jake's lip visibly curled. "If it were within my power, I'd shut down that whole department."

"Well, this might be the chance you're looking for," Nathan said, surprising Jake with his frank answer.

"I'm listening."

"Tom Wyatt is dead."

"Yes, I read that in the papers. Heart attack."

"Not a heart attack. He was murdered."

Jake's brow rose a fraction. "How do you know this?"

"Because I caught his body as a sniper buried a round in his skull. He was killed to shut him up just as Miko Archangelo opted to kill himself rather than face whoever is calling the shots behind the scenes. I don't have a way to prove it but I have a hunch that someone higher up the food chain is using ID as their own personal hit squad."

Jake's gaze narrowed. "And what would the motivation be?"

"If I were to take a guess? Greed. Tom was part owner of Tessara Pharmaceutical and as of the recent deal with Hashimoto Inc., it's worth billions. I did a hit on a man named Harrison Winslow—"

"The man the papers said was connected to the opium trade?"

He nodded. "The very same, but I don't think that was correct information. I think I was lied to about his guilt and it was to get Winslow out of the way of Tessara's deal with Hashimoto."

"Makes sense," Jake murmured, concerned. "Who else have you talked to about this?"

"Not many. The people with information keep ending up dead."

At that Jake paused and a ghost of a smile passed across his lips. "Well, it's a good thing you're hard to kill, right?" he said.

"Yeah. But my luck's about to run out without a little muscle behind me. You're above me in clearance. You can get into files that I can't."

Jake paused and then said, "You know you've given me enough information to shut down ID? You're good with that?"

Nathan didn't need to think hard on that one. Too many people dead and too many bad memories stuck in his head. "Yeah. It's time to turn out the lights. I used to think I was one of the good guys.... I don't think that anymore."

Jake nodded and climbed back into his car. "I'll be in touch." And then he pulled away, his tires echoing inside the underground garage.

Three days into her fake vacation, Jaci was ready to lose her mind. The first day she'd remained cloistered in her room, too terrified to venture out for fear of who might see her but on the third day, she had a raging case of cabin fever and needed to get out before she went insane.

The sugar-white, isolated beachfront property was a perfect hideout for someone who didn't want to be found. Quiet and peaceful, the place almost made her forget that her life had been tossed upside down and her heart was bleeding. It didn't take much to remind her—a scent, a memory, the sound of a man's voice too similar to Nathan's—and suddenly she was swamped by feelings of extreme remorse for agreeing to leave him. How stupid could she be? She shouldn't have been such a damn coward. So she'd seen a couple of dead people… Was that reason enough to run screaming in the other direction when the man she loved faced imminent danger? She had half a mind to climb in her car and head back to Los Angeles but Nathan's stern instructions to stay put always squashed her reckless impulse. He was right; she'd probably just get herself killed if she tried heading back but she hated not knowing if he was safe. He hadn't called—would it kill him to pick up a damn phone and let her know that he was okay? And her email was empty of anything but spam. She had no choice but to sit like a caught bird in a cage—a nice, pretty and mostly relaxing cage but a cage nonetheless.

She couldn't do this. Her brain needed activity. Jaci wrapped her sarong around her hips and padded barefoot back into the airy hotel foyer to use the hotel computer. She smiled at Alejandro and logged on using the complimentary Wi-Fi password.

She idly typed in Tessara to see what would pop up and not unexpectedly, news of Tom's death rose to the top but not ahead of the bigger news of megacorporation Hashimoto Incorporated offering to manufacture Tessara's newest wonder drug. She flipped through pages of news articles, nothing sparking a flame of curiosity, until she accidentally hit Images when she went to click on the URL bar to use a different search engine. There she found a photo that made her sit a little straighter. She zoomed the image. It was a group shot of the owners of Tessara, which included Tom Wyatt. She opened a new tab and cross-referenced Tom Wyatt to see if he popped up in connection with anyone else in the past and that's when she found success.

"It all goes back to Operation Sundial, I see," she murmured, double-clicking the old photo. There, standing arm in arm with a young Tom Wyatt, was a fellow soldier with the name that triggered her memory.

Penelope Granger.

"What have you been up to since your soldier days, Miss Penelope?" Jaci asked in a small voice as she did a search just for Penelope. It seems the woman had been busy since hanging up her military stripes.

But the most surprising find?

Her married name: Penelope Winslow, society matron extraordinaire and wife to one slain Harrison Winslow. Could the connection be as simple as a love affair gone wrong? Tom could have axed Harrison because he wanted to poach another's territory, but then why involve so many other people? Unless the risk was deemed worth it—as in worth billions?

Jaci gasped and jumped from her chair, causing the rattan to clatter to the tiled floor. "Are you all right, *señorita?*" Alejandro asked, alarmed. She jerked a nod and righted the chair, forced a bright smile and then babbled an excuse about needing a bathroom. She was too focused on reaching the burner phone she'd left in her room to realize she wasn't alone until it was too late.

Chapter 23

Jaci awoke with a sour taste in her mouth and a roaring headache. She blinked away the fuzziness and stared hard to reorient herself with her surroundings but she didn't recognize any of the posh furnishings. Gone were the rattan and cotton sofa and chairs. They were replaced with delicate French chairs with gilt edging and odd tassels hanging from the ends of the cushions. It was no doubt expensive and most certainly ugly.

Jaci rubbed her head and sat up slowly only to find a stately older woman sitting across from her, watching her with a faint amount of disdain. "Finally, she wakes."

Her tone delivered the message that Jaci's drugged slumber was somehow an inconvenience to her and Jaci couldn't help but snap, "Well, sorry I'm not used to being drugged and kidnapped. Next time I'll be sure to be a better hostage."

"Watch your tone with me," the woman warned coolly. "I could have every bone in your body broken in such a way that you remain conscious and alive but in the most wretched pain of your life. It's quite amusing to watch, I assure you. Should I arrange for a demonstration? No? Good, I really don't have time to play. Work calls and all that."

Jaci gulped and shook her head, making a mental note not to piss off the rich bitch in charge. "Where am I?" she asked.

"I'll ask the questions, if you don't mind." Her captor paused to regard her cuticle with a minute frown and for a moment, Jaci was deathly afraid for whoever had the misfortune of being her manicurist. "You've caused me a fair amount of aggravation," she continued, regarding Jaci with that pale, steady stare. She was really attractive, if you didn't mind the fact that her eyes reminded Jaci of a shark's eyes, not in color but in flat, cold ruthlessness. "Well, not you specifically, but your lover. He couldn't simply follow orders, now could he?"

"Harrison Winslow was your husband. Why'd you have him killed?" Jaci asked, cutting to the point. Her head was splitting and she was pretty sure the woman was going to kill her anyway so why not ask the burning question?

"Oh, so you know who I am?"

"Yes. Penelope Granger a.k.a. Penny Winslow. So

back to the question…why'd you do it? It seems you have plenty of money. Wasn't Harry giving it to you enough in the bedroom?"

"If you make another crude statement like that I'll have your tongue ripped out and fed to you. Am I clear? I learned a lot during my time in the military. Some lessons never leave you no matter how you might change on the outside." Penelope sighed dramatically as if she were the victim in all of this and said, "Do you know how much trouble I've had to deal with since your wretched boyfriend started poking around where he didn't belong? A woman of my stature has certain obligations and they do not allow for putting out the fires created by one redneck sniper who has outlived his usefulness. But Tom had a fondness for him. Damn him for being a sentimental fool."

"So it was always about the money?" Jaci asked and Penelope laughed at her look of disgust.

"Stupid girl, it's *always* about the money and anyone who tells you differently is lying. Harrison was never interested in selling to Hashimoto. He was a doddering old fool who cared more for his beakers and chemicals than he ever did for another living soul, including his wife. I put the money up for Tessara to start and with the help of an employee loyal to me, I procured the proprietary formula for the drug, Lovaz, and our team of scientists did the rest. Harrison was too stupid to see what was happening right beneath his nose. It was dreadfully easy to convince Tom that Harrison was dealing in opium and that he would be doing the world a favor by removing him."

"Was Tom dealing in opium?"

"Heavens, no. The man had no head for business—that was me." The beatific smile Penelope graced Jaci with sent a chill down her spine. The woman was a sociopath—a rich one, at that. "But when I could no longer convince Tom to send his drones out to take down some other meddlesome targets, and when he started babbling about perverting his position of power, I knew he'd become a liability. Such a shame. He was an excellent lover." She rose and straightened her impeccable satin blouse and said, "Speaking of lover...now we come to the point of this little tableau." A manservant came forward and on the silver platter was the burner phone Jaci had been desperate to reach before she'd been nabbed by Miss Psycho Socialite. "Time for you to call your boyfriend to arrange a meeting."

"And if I don't?"

Penelope laughed as if Jaci had actually cracked a joke. "You amuse me." Her smile faded and her gaze turned deadly. "Make the call."

"No."

Penelope drew a deep breath as if searching for patience. "No? All right then. Further motivation is required, I see." She motioned and the manservant came forward with a different phone. The screen showed a surveillance camera trained on James as he climbed into his car. "You'll never guess one of my favorite pastimes, something I picked up while serving abroad—

explosives. I just love the way they go *boom.*" She accentuated the word and Jaci's gaze widened in fear. Penelope's gaze narrowed with purpose. "Make the call."

Jaci accepted the phone with shaking fingers. "Don't hurt him," she pleaded softly. "You've already taken my best friend from me. Don't take James, too."

"*Darling,* don't make me," Penelope said as if Jaci were truly caught in a bad position, and Jaci wanted to beat her with one of the ugly chairs in the room.

Tears glittered in Jaci's eyes as she dialed. "Nathan? I'm in trouble."

Nathan's heart skipped a beat when he heard Jaci's voice on the other end of the line. He gripped the phone tighter. "Where are you?" he asked.

"I can't tell you. But I can tell you I'm *not* in Mexico any longer." She drew a deep breath and then continued, "I'm supposed to give you a message. Stop digging into business that doesn't concern you. If you agree to let bygones be bygones, and take a medical discharge from ID then you and I can walk away from this. If you don't agree to the terms, I'm dead and it's only a matter of time before you are, too."

"Are you hurt?" he asked.

"No."

"Tell your kidnapper I want to meet him face-to-face."

"Agree to *her* terms or this will be our last phone call."

Nathan swore under his breath even as his gaze narrowed at the valuable clue Jaci had dropped. He needed more time. He hadn't heard back from Jake and he'd run out of leads to chase. He was basically a lame duck at this point just waiting to get picked off and that made him very angry. "Fine," he agreed with a dark scowl. "I'll agree to the terms but you tell your kidnapper this—I have something she might want."

"What is it?"

"Tell her it's something Tom gave me before he died, something very valuable to Tessara. In fact, if I were to let this little memory stick fall into the wrong hands, I suspect the deal with Hashimoto would go down in flames."

There was a moment of silence and then Jaci said, "What are your terms?"

"A trade. You for the stick. And I name the meeting place."

"Those terms are acceptable. Where are we meeting?"

"The food court at the Galleria, over on Madison Avenue. In front of Giovanni's pizza place. Two o'clock."

She sighed as if irritated by something her captor said as she responded, "Unacceptable location. She's countering with Fleur de Lis on Buchanan."

Fleur de Lis was a fancy French bistro for elite customers who enjoyed overpaying for a wilted salad. "Fine," he agreed, his mind working at untangling the mystery of the location. Whoever was holding Jaci was accustomed to high-end service.

"One last thing—don't bring police."

"I won't bring cops. But I don't want flunkies showing up to do the exchange. I want to look the person in the eye who tried to ruin my life."

But before Jaci could answer, the line went dead. Nathan had no way of knowing whether the kidnapper had taken the bait but the fact that she was willing to meet him said she was worried that Tom might've had something of value hidden from them. God, Nathan hoped so. Because that's all he had to work with.

Nathan immediately placed a call to his brother, Jake. "We have a situation. Someone has kidnapped Jaci and they're threatening to kill her if I don't agree to their terms."

"What are their terms?"

"They want me out of the picture. They said they'd let bygones be bygones if I agree to a medical discharge out of ID."

"You know that's a lie, right?" Jake said.

"Yeah." Nathan remembered that Miko had also been offered a medical discharge. It was simply a way to get him out of the public eye and under the radar. "This is a one-way ticket. Chances are the minute my signature's dry on the paper of my resignation, by the next morning I'd be pushing up daisies."

"I made some calls and dug a little deeper into Tessara and found some interesting information. There's a common thread between Tom Wyatt and the wife of the late Harrison Winslow."

"Which is?"

"Penny Winslow served with Wyatt in a special ops mission called Operation Sundial back when they were young privates twenty years ago. The details of the operation are still classified but suffice to say, that they definitely have history. Something tells me Harry Winslow was unaware of that history and it might've cost him his life."

"Not to mention a landmark deal with Hashimoto," Nathan murmured, suddenly struck by a thought. "Penelope Granger was listed as one of the owners of Tessara.... Tom kept saying there was a woman calling the shots. This is starting to come together. I think the person we're looking for is Penelope Granger, or as she's known in more elite circles...society matron Penny Winslow."

"I'll make some calls," Jake said, his tone hard. "I have to tell you, Penny Winslow has some deep connections. If you're wrong about her...it's both our asses."

"I'm not wrong," Nathan said. "I'm willing to bet my life on it."

"All right, if you're sure. If you were anyone else, I'd tell you to come back with more evidence but you've never been one to exaggerate a threat. At least you didn't used to be."

"I know it's been a long time...but I haven't changed that much since we last spoke," he said quietly, remembering how proud he was when Jake had been accepted into the officer's training program nine years ago. Even though Nathan had done his part to help ease Jake's application through the proper channels, hard feelings had remained for Jake against Nathan for leaving him behind when Nathan split from home. Their father had taken out his rage on Jake and their mother had done nothing to protect him. Of course Nathan hadn't known and by the time he'd found out, the damage had been done. "Thanks for your help, Jakey."

"Don't call me that," Jake said brusquely. "I'll be in touch. Don't try to do this on your own. If Penny Winslow is to blame for what's been happening at ID, I need evidence, not *bad feelings* if I don't want to end up on the unemployment line beside you."

"Yeah, I got it," Nathan cut in, getting a little hot under the collar. "I'm no scrub and this ain't my first rodeo. You handle your shit and I'll handle mine."

"Good."

And then the line went dead. Nathan tossed his phone on the passenger seat and rubbed his forehead. Screw it. If his baby brother wanted to hold a grudge, that was his business, as long as he helped Nathan nail Penelope Winslow to the wall.

Chapter 24

Jaci tried not to fidget but she was woefully unschooled in the proper way to react to a hostage situation. If she weren't nearly dazed that she was in this situation at all, she might've laughed. Except there was nothing to laugh about. Jaci was nearly certain Penelope planned to have Nathan killed as soon as she had whatever Nathan was using as leverage. Something told Jaci that integrity and sticking to her word weren't truly ingrained in her. However, she probably took proper wine glass placement very seriously.

Penelope, Jaci and one of Penelope's men walked into the stuffy restaurant and were greeted by the host, an equally stiff and austere man who ducked his head in deference to Penelope as they crossed the threshold.

"Ms. Winslow, your regular table?" he asked in a deferential tone.

Penelope smiled yet her eyes were shrewd as she said, "Not today, Oscar. Today I would prefer a little privacy. I am feeling a mite puckish today."

"Of course. Perhaps the back patio would be more to your liking? I would, of course, see to it that you and your guests were not disturbed."

"Would you be a dear? That would be lovely," she said with clipped approval. Oscar smiled and led her personally to the lush gardenlike oasis of the patio dining area.

Penelope took her seat with a satisfied sigh and Jaci went to take the seat as far from Penelope as possible until the woman made a reproachful sound and looked pointedly at the seat beside her. "Don't be rude, darling. I don't bite," she said with a faint smile, which frankly didn't set Jaci's nerves at ease. The woman probably did bite. And often.

"I do love this place. It truly settles my nerves," she said conversationally as if they were there under completely different circumstances. Jaci glanced around, hoping to find some clue that Nathan was there and perhaps ready to jump out of one those ridiculously large potted plants, guns blazing. Alas, they were quite alone as far as she could tell.

Penelope's gaze narrowed as she said, "I remember when I still relied on men to save the day. The truth of the matter is, darling, men are only good for what is between their legs and rarely for what is between their ears."

Jaci swallowed the hot retort that jumped to mind before she said something that would cause Penelope to rip her eyelashes out for sport and simply waited for Penelope to finish her thought.

"I was once an idealistic girl, much like yourself. But I soon learned girls like that get used, forgotten or dead. Seeing as I didn't like any of those options, I started paying attention to people. Unlike men, a woman's greatest strength is her cunning. Men are such simpletons. Do you realize how easy it was for me to convince Tom to do my dirty work for me? Ah, almost embarrassingly easy. I'd really hoped for more of a challenge. But at the end of the day, it is what it is. Now I have enough money to buy all the men and firepower I need."

"You're a little bit crazy, you know that, right?" Jaci said, unable to help herself. "You can't go around killing people just because they don't fall in line with your agenda."

Penelope stared blankly. "No? And why not?"

Ugh. She couldn't argue ethics with someone who had none. "Never mind. I just want to get this over with. No more story hour, okay?"

Penelope's eyes turned mean as she said, "Carl… please encourage our guest to be more polite. Break her pinky finger." Before Jaci could react, the big man who had accompanied them snapped her pinky finger in one clean motion. The pain shot through her body and momentarily stole her breath. She gasped and cradled her injured hand. "See that you don't make a scene," Penelope advised her before taking a delicate sip of her Perrier. "I detest scenes."

"You're a psycho bitch," Jaci managed to grind out, blinking against the wash of tears stinging her eyes. "When Nathan finds out what you've done, there will be nowhere you can hide on this planet. He'll find you and rip your face off."

"It's amusing how you think that your boyfriend will save you. How do you know he's not dead already?" Penelope smiled and Jaci froze. "Perhaps I'm enjoying the anticipation of watching the hope I see in your eyes die when you realize no one is coming to save you."

"He's not dead," Jaci whispered, suddenly knowing it in her heart. "You're just crazy and spiteful."

"And what makes you so sure?" she countered, curious.

"Because I feel it in my heart that he's still with me."

Penelope's sudden flush of annoyance scared Jaci and she looked fearfully at the thug who'd broken her finger. "Balderdash and poppycock," Penelope finally muttered, angrily flicking a piece of lint from her tailored outfit before checking her diamond-encrusted watch. "Well, apparently your boyfriend is not the timely sort. Makes one wonder if he cares to show at all."

Jaci lifted her chin. "He'll show."

"Hmm...charming. So loyal." Penelope leaned forward, her eyes glittering with malicious light. "Did you know that your precious hero is nothing but a hired killer? The blood on his hands will never come out. Trust me, it doesn't matter how many good deeds you do, everyone will find a way to judge you for your minor slipups. I, too, used to save lives. It was the most boring aspect of my whole career."

"Don't compare yourself to Nathan. You're not in the same league."

"Of course not," Penelope agreed with a chuckle as if Jaci had said something quite amusing. "I am far *above* someone like your hillbilly boyfriend. To even suggest we are the same is beyond ludicrous."

"Yeah, because he's a true hero and you're nothing but—"

"Break her other finger, if you would," Penelope ordered her thug but this time Jaci saw it coming and leapt from her chair, grabbing a butter knife as she went.

"Come near me and I'll carve out your belly button," she hissed in warning, though in truth, she hoped he tried to rush her just so she could bury the knife in someplace soft.

"I told you I detest scenes," Penelope said, lifting her phone. "Need I remind you that a certain friend of yours is sitting dangerously close to an explosive device hidden beneath the undercarriage of his 1989 Ford Escort? The GPS tracking device says that his little blue dot is traveling down Magnolia Boulevard. One press of a button on my phone and suddenly, it's bye-bye computer whiz. Such a shame don't you think?

I've heard he's really quite brilliant. I have half a mind to offer him a job."

"I will not just sit here and let your thug break all my fingers," she said, her broken finger throbbing mercilessly. She couldn't stomach another. "And stay the hell away from my friends."

"Oh, fine. Stop being so melodramatic and sit down before you make a spectacle of yourself. I have a reputation to protect. The Red Hat Society, of which I've only just become a member due to the untimely death of my poor, sweet Harry, plays bridge here, you know. I'd hate to make a bad impression on my new friends," Penelope sniffed as if offended by Jaci's attitude and took another sip of her water. Suddenly her eyes registered someone entering the patio and Jaci's heart leapt in her chest—Nathan was here!

Nathan saw Jaci, cradling her hand, and he lifted his stare to the woman who was at the center of all this hell. He raised his hands to show he was unarmed and approached slowly. Jaci blinked back tears but remained quiet, her gaze flicking to the sharply dressed woman who was eyeing him with a pleasant but cool expression. "And you must be the *venerable* Nathan Isaacs, the hit man with a heart of gold," the woman said with a touch of derision. "Did you bring something for me?"

Nathan produced a small memory stick. "There's some good stuff on here."

Her smile turned brittle. "I can only imagine. Why

don't you share with me a preview of what's on that clever little device?"

"And ruin the surprise?" Nathan shook his head. "No, I think women like you could use a jolt now and then. Perhaps it will remind you of your humanity... and mortality."

Penelope dropped her smile and with it went her mask of civility. She snarled and held out her hand. "Give it to me."

His hand curled around the stick. "First, you and I are going to have some words."

Penelope's eyes glittered with open malice. "Would you care for a last meal? The caviar here is sublime. It's the least I can do."

"Are you forgetting something?" he asked, causing her to frown. "I haven't given you the stick."

"You will. And then I'll be done with this whole sordid business. You've been a thorn in my side for far too long and I'm ready to be finished with you. I became bored with your interference long ago."

"You said if Nathan agreed to a medical discharge from ID you'd leave us alone," Jaci reminded her hotly. "Aren't you a woman of your word, at the very least? Don't sociopaths hold anything sacred?"

Penelope graced Nathan with a knowing look and said, "Nathan knew the offer was bogus but he came anyway. He must really love you to sacrifice his life for you. Stupid man." A second thug appeared in an impeccable suit right behind Nathan. "Gentlemen, please escort Mr. Isaacs from the restaurant. *Quietly.*"

Jaci whirled on Penelope, her eyes wild. "What are you doing? You gave your word!"

"Yes, I did. How unfortunate for you that you believed me." She laughed but then she waved her hand in a seeming act of benevolence and said, "Go on, leave. I have what I want. You were never of interest to me. Nathan is the true prize. Leave before I change my mind." Jaci rose and looked to Nathan for guidance but when he simply nodded for her to go, her bewildered expression cut at his heart.

"As long as you're safe, that's what matters."

"Touching," Penelope said dryly. "It's simply too precious for words. The star-crossed lovers screwed over by fate. Boo-hoo."

"Cut the crap," Nathan said irritably, ready to put his fist through her perfectly lined lips. He'd never approved of violence against women but Penelope Winslow was testing that belief. "Jaci, go. Don't worry about me."

"You don't know what she's like," Jaci said, glancing at Penelope. "She broke my pinky finger just for saying something she didn't like. She's going to kill you!"

Penelope looked bored. "Can we move this along? I have other plans for this afternoon."

Nathan saw red at Jaci's admission and when he noticed her finger turning purple, he knew that it was indeed broken. But he couldn't tip his ace by letting his rage get the better of him. It was essential that she believe he was doing this to save Jaci. So much was riding on him being exchanged for Jaci. But if Jaci didn't get her butt in gear, she was going to ruin the entire plan. "Go! Get out of here," Nathan said tersely to Jaci, causing her to blink in wounded surprise at his tone. "Will you listen to me for once?"

"Fine," Jaci practically shouted, tears starting to stream down her cheeks. "You stupid, stubborn man. Have it your way! And when you wake up dead, don't come crying to me!"

Chapter 25

Jaci left the restaurant as quickly as her feet would carry her, her vision blinded by tears while her finger throbbed agonizingly. She didn't have time to go to the hospital and simply ignored the pain as her brain tried to figure out a way to save Nathan. The fool had sacrificed himself for her—always being the hero. There had to be a way that *she* could save *him.*

She ran to a phone booth on the corner but cried in frustration when she realized the handset was broken. Damn vandals, she thought, slamming the useless receiver back into its cradle. She didn't have a cell phone; she didn't have any money. She heard the distinctive rumble of the Metro bus as it pulled away from its scheduled stop and she ran after it waving her one arm wildly. When the driver slowed the bus so she could jump on, she pleaded with him to let her ride. "I've been mugged. My finger's broken and I need to get to the hospital. Can you please take me as close as you can?"

The driver, a big dark-skinned man with black moles populating his cheeks, glanced at her finger and she held up her hand so he could see the damage. He grimaced and nodded. "I can only take you as far as Shields. You'll have to walk from there," he said.

"Bless you! That would be wonderful. Thank you!"

Shields would take her close to her apartment. That was almost perfect. She slid into the nearest seat and wiped at her tears with her uninjured hand. An older woman with a kindly, soft face exclaimed when she saw the motley purple and black on her finger. "Oh, dear! What happened?" she asked, her expression filled with compassion.

Jaci closed her eyes and decided to stick with her story. "I was mugged. They took everything. My keys, my phone and my wallet. I need to get home so I can call my roommate."

"Well, honey, you can use my cell phone if you like," the woman offered. Jaci opened her eyes and almost started crying again at the generosity of the stranger. Penelope had nearly ruined Jaci's belief in people but this stranger had just renewed her sense that not all people were bad. She nodded gratefully and the older woman fished her cell phone out of her purse. "I hope they find who did that to you, honey. That looks dreadful."

"Thank you so much." Jaci quickly dialed the burner number and hoped and prayed that James picked up. Luck was on her side for James came on the line almost immediately. "Oh, thank God. James, something terrible has happened—"

"Where are you? Are you okay? I've been worried sick. Someone trashed our apartment. Whatever you do, don't go there."

"I'm fine, sort of. I don't have my phone or any money. Nathan's in trouble and we have to do something to save him before he goes and gets himself killed."

"Slow down. Where are you?" James asked.

"I'm on the Metro heading toward Shields."

"I'll meet you at Shields."

"You can't drive your car," she said suddenly, a new fear striking her. "Your car's been rigged to explode."

"Are you kidding me? That's not funny."

"Would I really joke about something like that?" she answered in exasperation. "I have a strange sense of humor but I would never joke about that. Please, be careful."

"Right. Thanks for the heads-up. I'll see you in a few."

Jaci returned the phone to the kind lady with a brief smile of relief and then leaned against the headrest with her eyes closed. She tried to ignore the pain in her finger but it was unlike anything she'd ever endured.

She could still see how everything had unfolded as if watching a movie featuring someone who looked a lot like her. He'd snapped her finger as if he were breaking a twig. It'd been efficient and done so quickly that she hadn't had time to react. God, that was so messed up. And she knew with a certainty that the first chance Nathan got he was going to kill that woman for hurting her. He might've overlooked a lot of things, except that. For the first time Jaci didn't feel conflicted about the level of violence Nathan experienced as part of his daily life. Somehow she just knew that it was going to end up saving both their lives.

Jaci hopped off the bus at Shields and thanked the bus driver profusely before running toward James. She stopped short when she saw another man with him. "Who is this?" she asked, not trusting anyone. But there was something about this man that was vaguely familiar, something that reminded her of Nathan. The angular jaw, the sharp gaze—she wasn't sure but it was something.

The man jerked a nod and said, "Get in the car. We'll talk while we drive."

Jaci scowled. He even talked like Nathan. Except the reason she tolerated that tone with Nathan was because she loved him. She didn't know this guy and he was already pissing her off. "First, you tell me who you are, and *then* I'll decide whether or not I'll get in the car with you."

"I'm Nathan's brother, Jake. Now get in."

Jaci shared a look with James of total confusion

and hopped into the passenger side while James took the backseat. Brother? "What are you doing here? Nathan said you lived in Florida. And why are you trying to help us?"

"My relationship with my brother is complicated. But I can tell you this—I've never lived in Florida and until this moment we hadn't spoken for nine years. He called me when you were kidnapped and told me what's been going on."

Nathan had lied to her? *Again?* Her lips felt numb. "How can you help us?" she asked, trying to focus on something other than the hurt. Would he ever trust her with his personal life? She swallowed, hating that she had more questions than answers. She cast James a wounded look for not warning her that he was bringing another person, particularly someone like Nathan's brother. She had to focus on the single most important detail right now or else she'd go insane. "We have to do something. She's going to kill him," she said with grim certainty. "I know this sounds over-the-top but she's evil and, quite possibly, unstoppable."

"No one is unstoppable. Not even the president of the United States."

Jake's confidence settled her nerves a little but the pain in her finger was becoming unbearable. Jake glanced at her injured finger. "There's a first aid kit in the glove compartment. Wrap your pinky finger against your ring finger and wrap it tight. It will stabilize the bone. Tell me everything you know about Penelope Winslow."

"When I was in Mexico, I discovered the link between Penelope Granger and Tom Wyatt."

"And how did you do that? I only just discovered it myself."

"Gotta love Google. I saw an old photo cached in Google Images."

"I swear, the internet is the biggest security breach in the history of America. Al Gore is probably rethinking his promotion of the World Wide Web back in the day right about now."

Jaci managed a brief smile before she started wrapping her finger, wincing as she wound the tape around. "But right after I made the discovery, I went to go call Nathan and I was kidnapped by Penelope's men right from my hotel room."

"And where did she take you?"

"I don't know," she answered, shaking her head. "They drugged me to bring me back over the border and when I woke up I was in a really fancy house with ugly furnishings. Looked like French Provincial to me but I'm no interior designer. My idea of couture is substantially more subdued than Penelope Winslow's."

"Does it look like this?" Jake held up his phone with a picture of Penelope Winslow standing in her salon, looking beautifully cultured and incredibly wealthy as part of a cover story on influential people in Los Angeles for a local magazine. Jaci nodded vigorously, recognizing every bit of furniture in that ugly room. Jake smirked. "I guess you're right. Google is a wonderful thing. Little Miss High Society broke a cardinal rule—never crap where you eat." Even as the discovery was a coup for them, his expression dimmed. "I have to level with you. There's a chance Nathan won't come out of this alive."

"What are you talking about? I thought you had a plan."

"We do have a plan. But that plan hinges upon Nathan getting Penelope to admit her part in Winslow's death and Tom's corruption of ID."

"And how's he supposed to get her to do that?"

"That's Nathan's problem. But if he can get her to talk that memory stick that he's got in his hand isn't actually a memory stick. It's a recorder."

"But recording someone against their knowledge isn't admissible in court. Her lawyers would chew that up and then she'd be out on the street again and just as pissed off as ever. Trust me, she is a psychopath in designer clothing with thugs who are very good at breaking things, such as human bones."

"Don't worry about that. Besides, we're not using the recording to prove our case in court."

"If you're not using the information to capture her, what are you going to use it for?"

"Let's just say, if it ever does go to court…it's a good line of defense."

Jaci stared. "He's going to kill her." At her flat statement Jake remained silent. She knew that was the likely outcome and possibly the only outcome to ensure their safety. But she would've rather seen the woman go to jail for the rest of her life. Somehow spending seventy years in orange polyester blend seemed far crueler than simply taking her out with a bullet. But, if that was the only way… "I understand," she said finally. "What can I do to help?"

"Just sit tight and let Nathan do his work. If Nathan doesn't get her to admit to her crimes, he's going to have to go to Plan B."

A shiver of apprehension followed as she asked, "What is Plan B?"

"You don't want to know."

Jaci stopped asking; she believed him.

"How early did you know that you were a sadist? Did you drown the family kitten or puppy?" Nathan asked, right before the thug landed another hit below his ribs. He grunted as the pain radiated but he wouldn't give her the satisfaction of him crying out. With each hit her smile grew wider. She was truly enjoying the show. "Did Winslow know of your secret life?" he asked when he could speak again, determined to make the pain worth something.

At that Penelope scoffed. "Harry was a dull academic too focused on his research than anything else. Do you realize that when I put the money up for Tessara, Harry didn't even ask where the money was coming from? He was too blinded by the opportunity to own his own lab to question where the money came from."

"I don't know. Why would he question? You're a

rich broad. Probably thought you had the cash in the rainy-day jar," Nathan said, wincing with every breath.

"Yes, well, be that as it may, I was getting tired of the everyday minutia of owning Tessara. Until I realized how much fun it could be to needle Harry. If all he loved was his precious laboratory, then I'd endeavor to make his life more interesting."

"How's that? Spike his morning coffee with a laxative creamer?"

Her lip curled. "Don't be crude," she said with a sniff. "I realized to make a game more interesting you have to involve more players. Quietly and under the radar, I became a silent benefactor for a small rival company and began feeding them information that would push them to become more aggressive in their research. With the right encouragement, my little pet project blossomed into quite a thorn in Harry's side. It became a game, to see how far I could push him before he'd notice that I was the one behind every victory with his rival company. He didn't find it the least bit curious that each time his scientists had a breakthrough, Tessara's scientists had an equal or greater breakthrough. But," she said with a shrug. "When Hashimoto became interested in Tessara, it ceased being a game and was just business. Honestly, if it'd remained a game I could have spent years torturing Harry, letting him have a few successes and then just when he had hope that his company might actually make something out of itself, I'd crush him again."

Penelope laughed, the sound a testament to her true evil. "Ah, Harry…I think I'll miss him."

"What about Tom? Will you miss him, too?"

Penelope stilled in reflection, finally answering, "Tom was a friend, a confidant and a lover. Of course I'll miss him."

"Then why'd you have him killed?"

Her eyes flashed. "*I* did not make that choice. Tom made that choice when he went soft. He used to be a soldier—a warrior! But then he started to buy into the hype of being a hero, being a *nation's* hero and suddenly he didn't want to kill people anymore." She actually pouted a little as if she were the victim and not the other way around. "I tried to explain to him that it was all the same—killing for personal gain or killing for his country's gain. Really, it's splitting hairs. And frankly I would rather line my coffers rather than Uncle Sam's. I cried the night he died."

"You mean the night you had him murdered?" Penelope's mouth tightened and she flicked a glance at her thug. Nathan absorbed the hit to his kidney and feared the impact might've sent it flying through to the other side of his body. "Truth hurts, doesn't it?" he gasped.

A cold smile spread across her lips. "You're one to talk about the truth. Being honest hasn't been your strongest suit, has it?" She switched tracks suddenly. "Why are you so interested in that useless girl? She's rude with no sense of style. And yet, you sacrificed yourself for her safety. Numerous times. Explain this to me."

"You wouldn't understand. You have to have a heart to get it."

"And you think you have a heart because you feel remorseful?" She leaned forward and pinned Nathan with a hard stare. "You knew Harry was guiltless when you pulled the trigger. You knew you were killing an innocent man and yet you followed through. Why? Don't bother answering. I already know. You justified the hit. You overrode your intuition and you did the job as ordered. That's a good soldier," she said with a hint of admiration. "I had high hopes for you. But that girl ruined everything. And now you're useless to me. I can't have a hit man with a heart of gold. I need a hit man who follows orders."

"In case you haven't noticed, lady, I don't work for you and I never did."

She laughed. "Really? And who do you think Tom was getting his orders from? Your last three jobs came from me."

"Prove it. I don't believe you."

"Samuel Chester. Charles Stanislaus. And finally Harrison Winslow." She chuckled. "If you had dug just a little bit deeper, you would've seen that none of them were a threat to national security. But they were certainly a threat to my empire. From opium fields in Afghanistan to marijuana crops in the San Fernando Valley—it's important for a lady to diversify her income stream. And each one of those men got in my way at some point or another."

She rose and walked toward him. He swayed on

his feet as his vision blurred from the sweat and blood dripping into his eye. Two thugs stood at the ready, their meat hooks clenched into fists. Her hungry gaze roamed his bare chest, clearly appreciating the hard ridge of muscle cording his abdomen. “It didn’t have to be this way you know. I’m a huge fan of your work and an even bigger fan of your physique.” She gave him a coy look. “I could ruin you for other women.”

Nathan didn’t hide his revulsion. “Lady, if you touch me, I’ll puke. Go ahead, I dare you. I had sardines and crackers for breakfast.”

“I like a man with fire. I could make you, you know.” She trailed a finger down his chest. “We manufacture a drug—under the radar, of course, because there’s no legal market for it—but it makes everything below the waist work and nothing above the waist. It’s like a date rape drug for women to use against men. Quite clever, actually. It’s my favorite.” Her smile brightened. “Should I show you? I would delight in riding your helpless body, forcing you to pleasure me.”

“Try it. The drug will wear off eventually and when it does, I will kill you the first chance I get. Doesn’t matter what you do to me, the time will come when I will exact my revenge. And not simply for what you’ve done to me but for what you did to Jaci.”

Penelope made a disgusted sound. “Ugh. Back to her? I should kill her and be done with it.” A different idea came to Penelope and her eyes lit up with promise. “Or I could make you work for me in *exchange* for her life. Isn’t that what you tried to do in the first place?

Set her free so that she would be safe? I could make that happen. If you agree to work for me *willingly,* I would ensure that she was never touched."

"The only problem? You're a liar and I would never put my faith in you."

"Such an angry man. So filled with manly passion. I find that highly alluring." She inhaled a deep breath as if loving the scent of his battered body and said "I'll give you some time to think about it. You have until this evening. If I don't get an answer I'll assume that you have declined my offer and before the night is through your girl will be bleeding on the street. You decide. Her life is in your hands."

Nathan glared at the woman, hating her. She exited the room with tinkling laughter. Plan B was sounding really good right about now. The two thugs approached him with vicious smiles. He eyed them without fear. "Time to play, boys? I'm ready. I should warn you, I'm out of your league and if you tangle with me, you will die."

The men both laughed at his warning. "We'll take our chances."

Nathan smiled, tasting blood on his tongue. "I was hoping you'd say that."

The first crunch of bone beneath his booted foot felt like sweet vengeance.

Chapter 26

Jaci couldn't help but steal a few glances at Jake, questions burning at the back of her brain as curiosity overrode her stern advice to herself to stay on task, but it was Jake who started asking questions first.

"How long have you known my brother?" he asked, as he methodically cleaned his gun.

"Not long. We dated for a few months."

"You must've really made an impression on him," Jake said, never taking his eyes from his cleaning. "I've never known Nathan to be so attached to any one person." She didn't know what to say to that. He seemed to realize his statement had fallen awkwardly between them and apologized. "That was uncalled for. I have some unresolved issues with my big brother," he admitted, adding stiffly, "I'm glad he met someone."

She nodded and tucked her lip beneath her front teeth, wondering how much Jake was willing to share. "Nathan told me a different story about your relationship. He said you lived in Florida. He never mentioned that you're in the same line of work."

Jake scowled, taking offense. "We are not in the same line of work," he corrected her. "I've never approved of ID's methods nor their shady, underground operations for the very mess Nathan is in now. There are no checks and balances, contrary to what they say, otherwise something like this never would've happened."

"So what do you do, then?"

"I work for the U.S. Department of Defense in Washington," he answered. "What?" he asked when he noticed Jaci's frown.

"James told me you work for a secret branch of the government that's pretty similar to ID," she said, not seeing the big difference. "Both departments are branches of the government that do things under the radar so as not to draw attention. I don't really see the difference."

"Well, it is different," Jake said, tucking his gun into his holster at his waist. "We have more paperwork."

At that tiny attempt at a joke, Jaci smiled. Jake was a lot like Nathan. She could learn to like him if he stuck around long enough. "So, what happened between you two?" she ventured.

"Old history. Not worth dredging up right now."

"I don't know… Seems like a good enough time.

You haven't spoken in nine years. I don't have any siblings but I always wanted one. Seems like having a brother would be like a built-in best friend."

He cast her a derisive look. "Not in the Isaacs family. We're not exactly the touchy-feely type. Growing up in our household was like sleeping in a war zone."

"Nathan told me your father was a jerk," she murmured. "But not much more than that."

"That's the highlight reel." Jake waved off the conversation, seemingly done with it. "Forget it—it's not really a great story. If Nathan didn't share details, there's no need for me to. Suffice it to say, it's no surprise we both split as soon as we were able. The miserable sons of bitches who laid claim to our biology didn't miss us when we split, either."

"I'm sorry," she said, hating how dismal their childhood sounded. "But at least you had each other. I would think that you would've clung to one another."

"Yeah...well, we were close for a time but that ended. And then life happened."

"Did you try to find him after you turned eighteen?" she asked.

"No," he answered with a clip, telling her she'd hit a nerve with the simple question. She was willing to bet there was a mountain of pain residing in Jake Isaacs, probably more than Nathan knew. He looked at his watch abruptly and stood. "I'm going to check in with my team before we move out. Stay put. I'll be back."

Jaci nodded. When this was all over—if they all managed to survive—those brothers needed to sit down in a room and hash out the past. She'd just have to make sure there were no sharp objects around when they did.

Jake needed a moment to collect himself as he stalked out of the room to shake off the black mood that had clouded his focus. He hadn't planned on sharing about Nathan but Jaci had a way of getting him to start talking, which was a total shock. Maybe that red hair gave her some secret mojo because Jake never talked about his past or his family.

When he'd received the call from Nathan after nine years of silence, he'd been tempted to tell him to find someone else to care because he sure as hell didn't. But for reasons he didn't understand, he hadn't told his older brother off and had grudgingly agreed to help.

To be fair, Nathan was in some serious hot water but more important, if Jake managed to bust open a corruption ring within ID, it would look mighty fine on his resume. So he couldn't say that his interest in helping was entirely grounded in familial loyalty and concern. Nathan had walked away from him nine years ago after helping Jake get into officer training school and hadn't looked back once. Not a phone call, not a letter. God, he'd begged Nathan to take him when he'd left home but Nathan had refused, saying he needed to finish high school. The memory still had the power to sting.

"You're leaving?" Jake had exclaimed in a scared whisper as Nathan had stuffed all he could manage into a ratty duffel bag. Nathan had nodded and Jake had jumped from his bed to start grabbing clothes, too, but Nathan had stopped him.

"You're not going," he'd said, scowling. "You aren't even old enough to drive yet. What am I supposed to do with you? You'd be listed as a runaway and everywhere we went you'd put a target on our backs. All it would take is one friggin phone call and the cops would be hauling our asses back to this hellhole. Sorry. Ain't gonna happen."

Panic had squeezed Jake's chest but he'd tried not to let it show. "So you're just gonna bail on me?"

"It's not like I have a choice. The old man is going to kill me or I'm going to kill him and I sure don't want to go to jail over him."

"And what do you think he's going to do to me when you're gone?" Jake had asked. "You can't leave me. If you do, you might as well just kiss my ass goodbye."

At that, Nathan had seemed ashamed that he knew Jake was right but he didn't change his mind. "Sorry. I can't worry about you all the time or I'll never get out of here. I'm joining the Marines as soon as I can, until then I'm going to lay low. Just do the same," he'd said, trying to offer some advice but Jake hadn't been interested in hearing it. He knew the score. As soon as their father learned of Nathan splitting, he'd take out his rage on his remaining son with no one to act as a buffer. His eyes had burned with childish tears; he was scared of losing his brother and being alone. Nathan had stopped at the window before climbing out, his expression grim. "Listen, I'll try to come back for you but it won't be right away, okay? Just stay strong and as soon as I'm able I'll try to get you."

Hope had blossomed in Jake's chest and he'd nodded. "Promise?"

There was a beat of hesitation and then, "I promise."

And then Nathan had slipped out the window and down the fire escape.

But Nathan had never returned and Jake had suffered unimaginable torture at the hands of his father until the day when Jake had thrown the old man up against the wall with murder in his soul and his father had realized the day had come when he could no longer bully his youngest son. Like Nathan before him, when Jake had walked out, he had never looked back again.

Until today.

Damn you, Nathan, for dredging up all those helpless, vulnerable feelings buried in the psyche of a young teenage boy. He wasn't that scared kid any longer but seeing his older brother after all that time had somehow awakened the pain all over again.

But somehow, walking away when his brother needed him hadn't been an option, even though Nathan had been able to walk quite easily.

Maybe if Nathan had known what Jake would suffer when he left, he would've taken Jake away with him. Maybe not. Hell, maybe it wouldn't have changed a damn thing. Nathan had never been accused of being overly sentimental. Frankly it surprised Jake that a woman had managed to pierce that hard shell tucked around Nathan's heart.

Lord knew he hadn't learned yet how to let someone in.

And, honestly, he didn't foresee that happening *ever.* Not with his line of work. What had Nathan been thinking to get cozy with a civilian? A civilian like Jaci, at that. He could understand perhaps the logic of hooking up with someone who was a solider or at the very least in the same type of work, but a graphic designer?

He drew a deep breath. Maybe he was jealous of what Nathan had, even if he didn't understand it. Jaci was a gorgeous woman and he actually liked her spunky style—when she wasn't driving him nuts—but he never would've picked her as a mate for his hard-nosed, no-nonsense brother.

But then who was he to judge? He'd never truly known his brother at all.

Chapter 27

Nathan sprang into the air, feet flying. His hands were bound but he didn't need his hands to inflict damage. Part of his specialized training included the use of his feet as deadly weapons. And it was too bad for the hired thugs that he outmatched them in both speed and skill. Blood sprayed as bones broke and within moments, he had subdued both men—possibly killing them. He didn't have time to care and simply worked to free his hands.

He removed a gun from one of the fallen thugs and then moved through the house with the stealth of a cat, his eyes and ears open for any sound. He needed that memory stick and he was willing to take his pound of flesh to get it. Preferably the flesh of that crazy bitch.

When he thought of Jaci's broken finger and how much it must have hurt, he saw red. In all of his years as a hit man and all the missions he'd accomplished, he'd never felt such unbridled rage. Emotion got you killed, that's what he always told rookies. But here he was, his thoughts consumed with one thought: find and destroy Penelope Winslow.

This was exactly what Jake had warned him about when they'd cooked up this plan.

"There's too much room for emotion, for screwing up," Jake had said, shaking his head, not liking the plan at all. "I think we should just call in some backup and hope for the best. Go the legal channel."

Nathan had scoffed at that idea. "Surely you're not that naive? You and I both know that a woman who has enough money and influence to do the things she's done is not going to quail at the threat of a subpoena. Besides, her lawyers would find a way to get her off scot-free. And that woman doesn't deserve anything less than a bullet or a life sentence. Preferably the bullet."

"I know it's hard for you to imagine, but there are rules for a reason. If she's guilty, justice will find her."

"I'm not taking that chance. I know she's guilty and I will see that justice is served."

"What, you think it's cool to be a vigilante? It's all about 'Nathan, being the badass,' isn't it?"

"You can shut the hell up because you don't know what you're talking about. This woman is a menace. Do you realize how many lives she's taken? She's out of control and if you don't have the balls to take her down, I will."

"I never said I didn't want to take her down. I just want to do it through legal channels."

"While I'm all for a plan that will work."

Jake's face had flushed with anger. "So what's going to happen if you lose your cool? Everything hinges on her admitting to her crimes. How do you suppose you're going to get her to do that?"

"I guess that's my problem, isn't it. You just keep Jaci safe. That's your job. And then when I've secured the memory stick, I will contact you and then you can ride in with your official team. I trust you can handle the *legal* part from there."

"Well, it's not going to help much if she's dead. I need you to keep your cool."

"I disagree."

Jake had continued, irritated. "We need her to give up her network of corrupt people. We don't know how far up the chain this goes so it's crucial that you bring her in alive."

Nathan had given Jake a hard look. Screw that. It wasn't his job to clean house. But even as he'd thought the uncharitable thought, he'd known it was unreasonable. Jake was right. If they could get Penelope to roll over on her network of corrupt associates, it could be a major win for everyone involved. "I'll do what I can, but no promises," he'd allowed grudgingly.

As Nathan rounded the corner he skidded as he nearly ran into another thug. He barely had enough time to react and block the hit before a meaty fist came barreling toward his face. Nathan ducked and countered with a hard uppercut, which knocked the man on his ass. Nathan didn't hesitate and brought his booted heel down on the man's windpipe, crushing it instantly. He didn't have the luxury of remorse or of hesitating—they'd picked the wrong side and now they were paying for it. End of story.

He burst through the atrium door and a loud shot rang out as a bullet buried itself in his midsection. He doubled over and fell hard to the floor, clutching his gut. *No!* It couldn't end like this. The pain was excruciating, radiating through his body like a sunburst of agony as the bullet ripped through something vital.

Penelope lowered the smoking gun and smirked. "You broke the cardinal rule, soldier. Never run blind into an open room." She approached him, smug. "Sloppy work, Nathan. I expected more from you. Truly, this is a disappointment. I would have thought that with your experience you would have been far more of a challenge. However, time has made you soft. And I'm ready to be done with you and all of your annoying interference."

She raised the gun and centered the shot at his forehead. "You know, I had thought of killing your girlfriend quickly for the sheer pleasure of snipping loose ends but then I realized I'd be cheating myself and so I want you to know, as you lie here dying, that when I kill your girlfriend, I will make sure that she suffers unimaginable pain before I finally snuff out her miserable, annoying life," she said, almost conversationally. "I think I will keep her alive for days, perhaps even tending to her wounds just so I can start all over again. The anticipation of watching her die is simply delicious."

Nathan funneled all of his wrath, all of his desperate desire to stay alive long enough to save the woman he loved more than anything, and found a burst of energy explosive enough to propel him up off the floor and into Penelope like a raging bull.

They fell to the floor and the gun went flying. She screamed and clawed at his face, and she drew bloody track marks down his cheeks as he grappled with the surprisingly strong older woman. He grunted and hit her hard with his elbow. She took the hit like a man, the blow glancing off her cheek but not slowing her down one bit. She landed a knee to his groin and he groaned as he rolled away from her. She scrambled to her feet and they both ran for the gun. He managed to kick the gun farther away and she snarled as she surprised him with a viper-quick snap of her wrist that nearly broke his nose. "You ought to put that down on your resume of special skills," he said, breathing hard as he wiped away the blood trickling from his nose. She grinned, her eyes glittering. "Wouldn't your high-society bitches like to see you now? Somehow, I think they'd be surprised at how truly vicious you are."

"You obviously know nothing about high society," she quipped, only mildly out of breath from their altercation. They circled each other warily as she added,

"Viciousness and cruelty are the hallmarks of any respectable well-bred family." She whirled and swung her leg in a perfect arc, narrowly missing his head by the thinnest of margins. "The problem with most women today is they don't appreciate the true value of staying in shape. Personally, I find martial arts training quite refreshing."

Nathan moved out of the way just in time before she swung around again and nearly took his head off with another arc of her foot. He stumbled on a small table, sending a vase to the ground, shattering. She quickly followed, vaulting the small furniture in her way. "Come on, now, when are you going to give me a run? This is almost too easy. Surely you had some kind of special training in all your years with the Marines? Perhaps you went into the wrong branch of the military. I picked up all sorts of valuable skills."

"I picked up plenty," he bit out, tucking into a roll, diving for the gun. His fingers managed to grab the gun just in time to aim and fire and Penelope crumpled with a scream as she crashed to the floor. He panted against the pain as his vision began to cloud. He was losing too much blood. He rolled to his feet and limped over to Penelope's fallen body. He nudged her with his foot. Her head lolled and she stared unseeing up at the ornate pressed-tin ceiling. "Seems my skills aren't as rusty as you thought, you psycho bitch." He winced as another wave of pain racked his body and he knew he didn't have much time left. He stumbled to the phone on the marble credenza and dialed his brother's number as he spied the memory stick. Penelope must have tossed it on the credenza, figuring she'd explore it later at her leisure. "I have what we need," he gasped, blinking hard to clear his vision, but it was no use. He gripped the phone harder, determined to finish the job right. "Send in the troops."

And then the black dots that had begun to swim before his eyes converged into one giant black hole and as his back hit the wall and he slid down to his feet he knew this was it. He didn't see a light, just darkness. He managed a sardonic grin. What had he expected, angels playing harps? No, he should have known all that was waiting for him at the end of the line was an endless sea of darkness and an eternity alone. Hell, it's what he deserved anyway.

Jake and his team entered Penelope Winslow's mansion and saw the dead bodies everywhere. But when he entered the atrium he saw Penelope Winslow staring off into space, quite obviously dead, and Nathan slumped against the wall, his hand covering a seeping wound in his gut.

Something twisted hard inside his own stomach and he sprinted to his brother's body. "Damn you, Nathan. I told you this would end badly." He checked for a pulse, knowing in his heart his brother was dead but when his fingertips caught the tiniest flicker of life pulsing stubbornly beneath them he leaped into action. He called for a medic, and a specialized ambulance service used only by certain branches of the government when a no-questions-asked policy was appreciated came within moments of the call. Nathan was placed onto a gurney and loaded into an awaiting ambulance while the rest of the team cleaned up the mess left behind. Just before leaving, one of the medics stopped and pressed something into Jake's palm. "We had to pry this out of his hand," the medic said. "I figured it must be important if he wasn't willing to let it go."

Jake stared and a slow smile crept across his face. His brother was one tough son of a bitch. Even near death, Nathan had held on to the most crucial piece of evidence they would need to save their asses: the memory stick. "Good job, big brother," he murmured, tucking the stick into his pocket.

That stick had the power to prove the fantastic claims Nathan had made against Penelope Winslow, otherwise, they might all be facing major prison time for killing the dear friend of several influential people in Washington, not to mention one of the most visible high-society matrons in Los Angeles.

Jake caught up to the medic and climbed in beside Nathan. It didn't feel right to leave Nathan alone after all he'd sacrificed. "How bad is it?" he asked, prepared for the worst.

The medic looked grim. "I don't even know why he's still alive. His blood pressure is nearly bottoming out and his heartbeat is erratic, but he's a fighter." The medic paused and when he saw Jake's expression, he assured him, "We're doing all we can for him."

"You do that," he said. "He's my brother."

As they rode, sirens blaring, to the hospital, Jake shuddered with an awful realization. If Nathan didn't make it, the task would fall to Jake to deliver the bad news to Jaci. And frankly he'd rather serve another tour in Afghanistan than do that.

Jaci might make him cry by talking about feelings and whatnot.

He looked to Nathan. "You'd better pull through this, buddy. I'm not kidding. Jaci's your problem, not mine."

Chapter 28

Jaci couldn't stop the tears. No matter how hard she tried to get them to stop, they simply leaked from her eyes as if on a mission to drown her in salty wetness. It was unnatural to see Nathan lying there in that hospital bed, so still, hovering between this world and the next as his body fought an epic battle to stay alive.

"Don't you dare die on me, Nathan," she murmured, wiping away tears. "This isn't fair. You've only just come back to me and now you're trying to leave again. If you die, I will follow you into the hereafter and drag your sorry ass back so if you don't want to be embarrassed in heaven or hell or wherever you're going to end up, you'd better get your butt back to me because I'm not going anywhere until you do."

All of her dreams and hopes of a future with Nathan seemed so far away as the steady blip-blip of the monitors reminded her that at any moment, fate could pull him away from her. His injuries were grave—the doctors had given him a less than thirty percent chance of survival—but somehow, he continued to defy the odds by making it to another day.

When she and Nathan had first started getting serious, she had daydreamed about a big fancy wedding, inviting all of her design clients to this grand gala, looking like a princess in a fairytale as she floated down the aisle to her handsome prince.

But now? After everything that'd happened, all she wanted was Nathan. She didn't care about the big wedding, she didn't care about backyard barbecues with the neighbors and she didn't care if they never had a little house with a cute white picket fence. She just wanted Nathan, alive and in her life.

She was not the same person she was a mere week and a half ago. Since meeting Nathan, her life had changed in so many ways. She was stronger, more sure of herself and she knew more than anything that she loved Nathan in a way that didn't seem possible to feel for another human being. It was the kind of love that made or broke people. She knew this because losing him the first time had felt like losing a piece of herself.

And now that she was standing here, staring down at his battered and abused body as he fought to live because he'd done something incredibly brave and stupid, she wanted to hold him close and never let go. The bottom line was, she would take Nathan any way she could have him. And if it meant that they had to traipse around the world, a new zip code every few months—or new identities—she didn't care. None of that mattered. And the fact that in the past she thought it had just went to show how naive she'd really been.

When she thought of herself and Sonia stumbling down that dark alley, oblivious to the danger that was heading their way, she bowed her head at her own foolishness. It had been her idea to take the back alley when the street would've been safer; it had been her stubbornness that had cost her dearest friend her life. And if Nathan hadn't drugged her silly butt, she would've allowed that stupid sense of righteous indignation to put an end to her days for she surely would've been next.

Nathan had braved her rage, her hurt and her condemnation to ensure her safety and she didn't know a man alive who would've done the same. Simply put, Nathan was her everything—just as she was his. The irony that she could finally recognize that plain truth at such a bleak hour was grief and fear at its most poignant.

She heard a shuffling sound and turned quickly to see James at the door, who was unsure if he should enter. "I know I'm not family, but I just wanted to see how he was doing," he said quietly, adding with something akin to surprise in his voice, "I kinda like the jerk. He's not really the sort of guy I would hang out with under normal circumstances but I respect him and he plainly loves you, so he can't be all bad."

Jaci gestured with a smile for James to come in. "I think if the situation were different, you guys might have liked each other. Yes, on the surface you're totally different but you're both passionate about what you do. He might not understand computer stuff and you don't understand violent secret government stuff but you both share the same tenacious spirit."

James grinned, accepting the compliment. But after a moment he sighed and confessed, "You know, I have to admit, when you asked to move in with me after your breakup my reasons weren't entirely altruistic. I've had a thing for you for a long time but the fact of the matter is, I'm not the right guy for you. When I saw you with him, I saw you light up with a glow from the inside. I guess I never believed in all that soul-mate love stuff but you proved me wrong." He exhaled a deep breath and added with note of chagrin, "Of course, now that I know soul mates exist, I have all this pressure to go find mine. Hopefully, she likes computers and spreadsheets and formulas, otherwise we're going to start on a rocky foot."

Jaci smiled, her eyes watering. "When you find the right woman, it won't matter if you're completely different or exactly alike. All that will matter is how you feel when you're with her. But I know you'll find an amazing person, James, because *you* are amazing. And even though I'm not the right one for you, I know that she is out there. You're just too good of a man with an incredible heart to spend life alone."

James ducked his head as if embarrassed, but she

knew that he took her words to heart. They'd been friends for too long and they valued each other's opinion. "I know he's going to make it," he said, surprising Jaci with his sudden assessment.

"What makes you say that?" she asked.

"Because that man loves you. And there is no way he could live without you. Even if you drive him crazy."

Jaci laughed, wiping away tears. "Maybe. I hope so. The doctors have done the best they can to repair the damage. But he lost a lot of blood. Thankfully Jake is the same blood type and he was able to donate a pint for Nathan. All we can do now is wait."

"I can wait with you," James offered.

"I'd like that."

"So…Jake and Nathan… There's a story, right?"

Jaci sighed and smoothed a lock of hair from Nathan's forehead. "I don't know all the details but I know they've got a lot to work out. I like Jake, though. I hope they can put the past behind them."

"If I know you, you're going to make that your priority. Well, your priority once Nathan is in the clear."

Jaci smiled at James's accurate assessment. Family was too important to throw away, especially when you had precious little of it. Nathan and Jake had to work out their differences. Jake cared about his older brother, even if he didn't want to admit it; his actions proved it. And Nathan knew his brother had been the one person who wouldn't let him down, in spite of their nine years without contact. She'd gladly take on the role of mediator to mend that rift.

But first…Nathan had to pull through.

She leaned forward and brushed a tender kiss across his brow. "Please come back to us, baby. We're all waiting for you," she murmured and squeezed back tears. *Please.*

Nathan floated through a sea of nothing, unaware of pain or pleasure. But a face floated through his consciousness like a beacon of light that beckoned and flirted and enticed him to follow. When he lost sight of that beautiful face, when the darkness enveloped and obliterated all trace of her features, he heard her voice whispering in his ear, calling his name. And when he couldn't hear her voice, the scent of coconut and cucumbers teased his senses and tugged at his body until he had no choice but to follow. He didn't know who she was but he knew somehow that she represented safety and home. Her voice warmed the cold cockles of his heart and her familiar scent chased away the fear crouched in his mind.

He heard the sound of her voice again as it penetrated the blackness and he rested as the sound flowed over him in a sweet caress. He could listen to her all day. He didn't know what she was saying and it didn't matter. It was the cadence of her voice that washed over him, wrapping him in a feeling of love and contentment. Was this heaven? He didn't know, but he didn't want to leave if it meant leaving that voice behind.

But something—and he wasn't sure what—made him realize that he couldn't stay in that oblivion forever. Something outside of this place awaited him. He became restless, no longer content with the darkness and the weightless freedom of his body. He wanted to know more about the sweet voice and the hair that smelled of cucumbers. Who was that woman? Jaci, a voice whispered. Yes, he thought. That was her name. And he loved her.

He pulled memories from his sluggish brain and focused until he could see them more clearly in his mind. He saw her laugh, the way her mouth opened with abandon as she heard a good joke; the way she bit her lip when she was nervous. Her red hair with the gold highlights glinted in the sun and her green eyes made him think of polished jade. Memories began to come back to him. Memories that weren't as sweet or soft or smelling of cucumbers.

He remembered blood and gore. And rage.

He remembered lives he'd taken. He remembered justifications he'd made and now regretted. He saw a lifetime of messed-up choices—except for one: the choice to chat with a beautiful young woman in a coffee shop. That had been the best decision of his life.

Now he had to get back to her. He needed her the way his lungs needed air. He would die for her—gladly. But if he had a choice, he'd rather live his life beside her. He wanted to put his children in her belly; he wanted to watch her grow old. He wanted to do all of the things that he'd never dreamed possible for a man like him. He wanted it all with Jaci. He wanted to give her all of the things she deserved but most of all he wanted to freely give her something that she'd breathed life into from the moment they met. His heart had started beating a rhythm made only for her. She'd stolen his heart that day in the coffee shop; it was time he told her.

This time when he heard her voice filtering through the black cloud that surrounded him, he followed the sound. He followed it all the way until he was free from the dark oblivion. He slowly became aware of his body, and the myriad of aches and pains that collided into a symphony of agony nearly sent him running in the opposite direction. He gritted his teeth, determined not to shy away from the pain.

On the other side of that wall was the woman of his dreams. He would do anything for her. Suffer any amount of pain if it meant he could spend the rest of his life with her. He didn't deserve her love but she didn't care and she gave it to him anyway. Without Jaci, life wasn't worth living.

His dry and parched lips moved as he tried to pull the feelings from his heart to form into words but he was simply too weak. He tried again. *Just say the words,* he told himself fiercely. It mattered. *She needs to hear how you feel. How you've always felt, since the day you met. How you knew without a doubt that it didn't matter what happened between you from that moment forward, that nothing would ever change.* She had stolen his heart with one glance from those beautiful green eyes. She hadn't known it then but Nathan had known and the knowledge had both fascinated and terrified him. *Say it! Make it happen.*

"I love you."

The words were but a whisper and as his bleary eyes sought to focus on her face, he heard her sharp intake of breath and the sudden pressure of her hand against his cheek as she leaned forward. "You're alive," she said, tears of open relief choking her voice. "I've been waiting days for you to open your eyes, so scared that you were gone forever." Wetness splashed his cheek and he realized she was crying. He would do anything to wipe away her pain. "Say it again," she whispered, nuzzling his cheek. "Say it again, Nathan."

He would happily say it for the rest of his life. "I love you, Jaci," he said, his voice hoarse and barely a note above a murmur. "I love you."

Her shoulders shook as she brought his hand to her lips, saying fervently, "I love you, too, Nathan. Please never leave me again."

"Not even death can keep me from you."

"Promise?"

"Promise."

She sealed her mouth to his and he wished he had the strength to clutch her to him with all of the fierce, raw emotion cascading through his heart but he knew they would have plenty of time for that in the future. As his eyes fluttered shut as pure exhaustion took over, Nathan knew his life was never going to be the same.

And for the first time ever, he wasn't simply looking forward to the future with grim determination to succeed or conquer. He was going to live it with pure joy. And that, he knew, was going to be the grandest adventure of his life.

Epilogue

Azure seas stretched for miles across sugar-white sand as gulls wheeled and cried from above, the tranquil sound of waves breaking and lapping the shore as soothing as a smooth glass of wine after a hard day. It was amazing how perspective made a difference. The last time she'd stayed at Casa en el Mar, Jaci had been scared out of her mind and worried about Nathan. But this time? She didn't have a care in the world.

Nathan's hand circled her waist seconds before his mouth traveled a sensual line up the column of her neck. She smiled dreamily and leaned into his touch. The balmy air of the Mexican beach caressed her skin and she sighed with pleasure. "How did you know where to find me?" she asked, playfully, as she turned and looped her arms around his neck. "I thought you were going to rest for a bit?"

"Well, someone once told me that to find you, all I had to do was look for the girl wearing the green-striped bikini," he answered with a sly grin. "I'm just glad it was you. Imagine how embarrassed I'd have been if you'd been someone else."

She gasped at his joke and he squeezed her behind with bold suggestion in his eyes. She caught her breath and her tongue darted out to wet her lips. "You're supposed to be taking it easy. The doctor said no strenuous activities."

"I guess I'll just have to let you do all the work," he said with a devilish grin that liquefied her resolve.

She smiled, not minding that idea at all. "You're incorrigible," she murmured against his lips, then added, "But I like that quality in a man."

His grip tightened on her behind. "And I like when my lady likes to bend the rules," he said. She thrilled at the subtle hint of possession in his tone. Oh, goodness, she liked a little caveman attitude in her man. She grinned up at him boldly. "So what are you waiting for? This bikini isn't going to untie itself."

Quicker than she ever thought possible for a man recovering from a bullet wound to the stomach, Nathan undid the ties to her bikini top and held the tiny scrap of green material dangling from his hands. His spreading grin said he liked what he saw. She gasped and tried to cover her breasts, all the while trying to grab her bikini top. "What are you doing?" she squealed with embarrassed laughter. "You crazy man, give me back my top."

"If it were up to me, this is how you would walk around all day. Lucky for you, we are the only guests here. So how about we say we take off those bottoms, too."

He reached for the tiny strings and she danced out of reach. "If you want these bikini bottoms off you're going to have to catch me first," she exclaimed as she sprinted for their cabana. Even recovering, Nathan had the speed of an NFL athlete. But perhaps she was guilty of slowing her speed just enough so that he could easily catch her. The truth was, Nathan could coax her out of her clothes anytime and anywhere.

She supposed that was just one of the many perks of being engaged to the most wonderful man on the planet—a man she simply knew as her soul mate.

* * * * *

COMING NEXT MONTH FROM

HARLEQUIN®

ROMANTIC suspense

Available October 1, 2013

#1771 KILLER'S PREY

Conard County: The Next Generation
by Rachel Lee

After a brutal attack, Nora Loftis returns to Conard County and the arms of Sheriff Jake Madison. But her assailant escapes, and he's coming for her. Can Jake protect her and heal her soul?

#1772 THE COLTON BRIDE

The Coltons of Wyoming • by Carla Cassidy

Heiress Catherine Colton broke rancher Gray Stark's heart, but when danger surrounds her, he steps up. A marriage of protection will keep her safe, but he finds his heart at risk.

#1773 TEXAS SECRETS, LOVERS' LIES

by Karen Whiddon

With her best friend missing, Zoe risks her life to find her, but she can't do it without Brock McCauley, the man she left at the altar five years before—and never stopped loving.

#1774 THE LONDON DECEPTION

House of Steele • by Addison Fox

When a sexy archaeologist teams up with a mysterious thief to unearth a cache of jewels in Egypt, the competition turns deadly and the only person either can trust is each other.

To unearth a cache of jewels in Egypt, a sexy archaeologist teams up with a mysterious thief from her past.

Read on for a sneak peek of

THE LONDON DECEPTION

by Addison Fox, available October 2013 from Harlequin® Romantic Suspense.

Rowan wasn't surprised when Finn followed her into the elevator, but she hadn't counted on his rising anger or the delicious sensation of having his large form towering over her in the small space.

"I can explain."

"I sure as hell hope so."

"Rowan. Listen—"

"No." She waved a hand, unwilling to listen to some smooth explanation or some sort of misguided apology. "Whatever words you think you can cajole me with you might as well save them." The elevator doors slid open on her floor and she stomped off.

She was angry.

And irrationally hurt, which was the only possible reason tears pricked the back of her eyes as she struggled with her electronic key.

"Here. Let me." Finn reached over her shoulder and took the slim card from her shaking fingers. The lock switched to green and snicked open.

She crossed into the elegant suite and dropped her purse on the small couch that sat by the far wall, dashing at the moisture in her eyes before he could see the tears.

"Rowan. We need to talk."

"You think?"

"Come on. Please."

She turned at his words. "What can you possibly say that will make any of this okay?"

"I couldn't tell you."

"You chose not to tell me. There's a difference."

He was alive.

The young man who she'd thought died saving her was alive and well and living a life of prosperity and success in London.

"Do you know how I've wondered about you? For twelve long years I've wondered if you died that night. I've lived with the pain of knowing I put you in danger and got you killed."

"I'm fine. I'm here."

"And you never even thought to tell me. To contact me or give me some hint that you were okay. That you'd lived."

"It's not that easy."

"Well, it sure as hell isn't hard."

HRSEXP0913

Love the Harlequin book you just read?

Your opinion matters.

Review this book on your favorite book site, review site, blog or your own social media properties and share your opinion with other readers!

Be sure to connect with us at:
Harlequin.com/Newsletters
Facebook.com/HarlequinBooks
Twitter.com/HarlequinBooks